SHOWDOWN IN MAGIC CITY

SHOWDOWN IN MAGIC CITY

MAGIC CITY CHRONICLES™ BOOK FOUR

TR CAMERON   MICHAEL ANDERLE   MARTHA CARR

For those who seek wonder around every corner and in each turning page. And, as always, for Dylan.

— TR Cameron

To Family, Friends and
Those Who Love
To Read.
May We All Enjoy Grace
To Live The Life We Are
Called.

— Michael

Ruby Achera, her sister Morrigan, and her shape-shifting partner Idryll crept across the three-story high rooftops in the warehouse district south of Ely, Nevada, concealed by illusion and their usual disguises. She'd received the tip from Sheriff Alejo earlier, courtesy of her source among those selling magical black-market items in Magic City, that something was going down that night. The sheriff didn't have confirmation of *where* it was going down, though, so following the informant was the only way to find the location. They paused at the edge of a roof, waiting to see what their quarry on the sidewalk below would do next.

Morrigan complained, "This is boring."

Ruby snorted. The other woman's clear voice came through the earpieces set in the magical mask she wore, after its upgrades by a friendly technician. "Quit whining. You're here by choice. Besides, there will be fun soon enough."

Idryll, sounding decidedly superior, said, "Maybe you

two could focus on work for a moment? He's entering that building."

Ruby replied, "For someone who spends more than half her day pretending to be a house cat so she can sleep without being bothered, I don't think you're one to lecture others about professional behavior." Her sister opened a portal from their current position to the other roof and waved them through. Had Morrigan not come along, they would've had to use magic to leap from one building to the other since Ruby couldn't create a portal to a place she hadn't physically been. *One of the fun things about being me.*

She quietly crouch-walked to a small skylight despite being covered in a veil of illusion that would hide her from eyes and ears. Idryll's claws easily pried it open, and Ruby let herself down into the rafters, then slithered sideways so the others could do the same. Below, the warehouse floor was a bustle of activity as dwarves, Kilomea, and at least one elf shifted boxes to clear the space for the shipment to come. "I'll take the near corner. Morrigan, all the way across opposite me. Idryll, you have the middle."

Her partners replied in the affirmative and moved, Ruby segmenting one part of her attention to preserve the illusion wrapped around the tiger-woman. While her partner could move in complete silence, given her feline nature, it was always possible that someone might look up at an inopportune moment. *Besides, what's the point of having the ability if you don't use it?* She made sure her own aural and visual concealment was solid, then muttered, "Connect Alejo." A soft *bing* signaled an active connection. "He led us to a warehouse. They're in here, as expected. You solid?"

Valentina Alejo was Ruby's best ally—*okay*, only *ally*—among the law enforcement that watched over Ely. Ruby didn't trust the city's local police, figuring criminals with deep pockets probably had someone on the payroll, or possibly the department simply leaked like a sieve because they couldn't afford sufficient security. Either way, they weren't on her list of reliable resources. The other woman's voice was on the low end of normal and a little gravelly with adrenaline. "Yeah, we have it. Apparently, they don't let their workers know which warehouse they're headed to until they're en route. Clever operational choice. Bastards."

"Paranoid, but effective."

The sheriff gave a derisive snort. "Fair enough. Guess we're not dealing with total idiots, unfortunately. What do we have inside?"

"Magicals, probably a dozen or so. A few humans, unless they're in disguise."

"Okay, let's proceed as planned. When the truck is in, we'll wait a couple of minutes for things to get moving, then order them to surrender. If they do, all your hard work preparing is for nothing."

Ruby shook her head. "I don't think the odds of that are particularly good."

Alejo grunted. "Me neither, which is why I asked you to join. If they choose any option other than standing down, do your thing. We'll stay out of your way unless you call us to come in and help."

"Got it. See you soon." She killed the external connection and reported, "Plan stands. Remember, we need to be completely nonfatal. We're working with the police on this one. They can overlook bruises and broken bones, but if we step over that line, we become the bad guys."

Morrigan replied, "Seems unfair. Those scumbags below won't pull any punches."

Idryll chuckled. "Consider it a testament to your incredible aptitude."

Ruby's and Morrigan's replies overlapped. "Shut it."

The sound of the huge garage door sliding up on its tracks and a truck rolling in forestalled further conversation. It was twenty feet long or so, a rental, bright yellow and covered in scratches, dings, and dents. As soon as it was inside, the people below surged into motion, hitting the switch to close the door and using magic to begin pulling crates and boxes from the vehicle. Ruby breathed, "Damn, that's a big truck. They must have a lot of stuff. Who would've thought little Ely was such a nexus of criminality?"

Morrigan asked, "Have you been paying attention lately?"

She ignored the comment. "Okay, looks like our initial plan will work pretty well. I'll take out the ones at the back of the truck, Idryll jumps on the top and engages targets of opportunity, and Morrigan, you protect the informant's identity."

Her sister confirmed, "On it. I don't think he's going to thank me for it."

Ruby shifted to get a better angle on her assigned criminals as she replied, "From what I understand, he's a scumbag who got a deal. He deserves whatever he gets. Still, maybe no permanent damage, so he can continue to be useful?"

"I'll consider it."

A series of resounding *clangs* came from the metal garage door, followed by Alejo's voice through a megaphone's mechanical distortion. "You inside the warehouse. This is Sheriff Valentina Alejo. Open the door and get on your knees with your hands on your heads." The reaction was instantaneous and not compliant. The thugs below took positions facing the entrance, clearly ready for whatever fight the authorities wanted to bring to them.

Bad choice, chuckleheads. Ruby said, "Game faces. Going in ten seconds." She ticked the time off in her head as she pulled a grenade from her belt. It was about the size of her palm and contained magical electricity that would discharge on impact. She'd made it herself and was pleased with the results, although she looked forward to working with Margrave to improve it. When her mental timer ran out, she dropped the disc at the back of the truck. Her hand was already in motion for another weapon, one of her techno-magical mentor's concealment grenades, and she had it ready when the first went off.

The trio of dwarves below shuddered and jerked in the grip of the arcane lightning. Two of them collapsed, while the third, apparently hardier than the others, remained standing, wobbling in place. She dropped the next grenade to protect her descent and jumped.

As soon as Morrigan saw the object fall from Ruby's position, she released her arrow. It sped true to its target, the dwarven informant who stood nervously to one side of the warehouse, notable by his immobility. His hair was mussed as if he'd run hands through it, and the stress of his situation showed on his wrinkled face and in his anxious bearing. The missile slapped him in the chest and wreathed him in magical lightning. He jittered for a moment before falling senseless to the concrete floor.

Morrigan was already nocking her second projectile, which she loosed into the middle of a trio of nearby enemies. It struck one in the shoulder and released a cloud of billowing white vapor. Her target fell immediately, but another reacted quickly to create a wave of force that pushed air in front of it, lifting the knockout gas back toward her position. While the filter built into her magical mask would handle it easily, the action proved her cover was blown. She hit the button to collapse her bow into its baton form with her left hand while simultaneously grabbing a disk on her belt with the right. She tossed the concealment grenade at the floor and leapt after it.

Idryll delayed through the initial flurry until her partners had released their magical smoke grenades. Clouds billowed up and around from both positions, blocking both magical and mundane senses. She threw hers to the far side of the warehouse as a distraction and dropped from the rafters to the roof of the truck below. Her landing wasn't soundless, thanks to the groan of flexing metal as her weight hit it, but in the cacophony of yells and screams that accompanied the unexpected attacks from above, her move went unnoticed.

She'd been tracking the trio of Kilomea positioned throughout the warehouse, naturally interested in engaging the most dangerous opponents available. A somersault took her off the top of the truck and feet-first into the nearest hulking figure's chest. Even in humanoid form, she massed more than her size would suggest, and the strike knocked him backward. She landed cleanly and pursued his involuntary retreat, extending her claws then retracting them again as she remembered Ruby's warning.

A pair of punches slammed into his chest, right where her boots had hit, and his pained expression revealed she'd probably broken a rib. Still, the giant creature was roughly two feet taller, twice as wide as she was, and born and bred for battle. *That makes him almost a worthy foe.* He punched with his left, and she ducked and bobbed her head to the side. Fortunately, she'd moved away from his other arm, which whipped around with a pair of heavy, reinforced metal bands over his knuckles leading the way. She let herself roll into a backward somersault to avoid it and heard the sizzle of electricity as it passed. *Oh, he brought toys. Lovely.*

She bounded up at the end of her move and tried a kick to his head, but he smashed her leg aside with a block that felt like a punch and followed up with the knuckles again. She didn't get out of the way quickly enough, and electrical energy blasted through her, setting her nerves on fire. A small yelp escaped as she stumbled to the side. "Ow. Bastard. You'll pay for that."

Her muscles wanted to shut down, but she wrestled them under control with a discipline instilled by long experience. Her foe waded in with a smile, thinking he had her number. She let him get close and flowed out of the way of the left that was the distraction, positioning herself for the right cross. He threw it. *First mistake.* He put his whole body weight behind it, going for the killing blow. *Second mistake.*

The shapeshifter stepped in and grabbed his wrist with her right hand, spinning to smash an elbow into his face. The smart response would have been to retract the arm immediately and retreat, but he didn't. *Third mistake.* She spun back in the opposite direction and used his wrist as a lever, locking it out and jerking him down to his knees, his only other option being to let the joint break. *Fourth mistake.*

Idryll wrenched the wrist and snapped it anyway, then yanked on it to position his head for an ax kick. She lifted her leg and brought it down on the back of his skull, using less force than she would have if the police hadn't been present. He went down, dazed, and she grabbed his hand and pressed it against his neck, where the knuckles discharged with a loud *snap*. He shuddered, twitched, and fell unconscious. She straightened, flicked her head back to get her long hair—normally orange and black, but now pure black in the mask's disguise—out of her face. *Okay, who's next?*

CHAPTER TWO

Ruby dropped cleanly, using a small burst of force magic at the end to buffer her landing. She spun instantly into a roundhouse kick to the head of the dwarf that hadn't succumbed to her electrical attack, laying him out on the concrete floor of the warehouse. The place was chaos, with people running around shouting commands and yelling in alarm.

A scuff from behind warned her of an enemy. She crouched and launched a spinning no-look leg sweep in the direction of the noise. The Kilomea responsible for the sound hopped over her attack with unexpected nimbleness and threw a kick in response. She rolled to the side and came up to her feet while reaching for her sword. She drew it and slashed it down at his collarbone, releasing a tendril of force magic to coat the weapon and turn it into a bludgeoning implement rather than a cutting one. He blocked it with a circling motion that put the flat of his hand against the blade, a fearless move she couldn't help but admire. His other fist snapped out at her face, and she leaned backward enough that it failed to connect.

Ruby grabbed his wrist with her free hand, but he pulled the arm back and swiveled into a punch with his right. She blocked, counterattacked with the hilt of her weapon at his nose, and he blocked in return. They traded several blows, then his speed suddenly increased. *He must be using magic to boost himself. That's fine. Two can play that game.* She hadn't yet mastered that particular technique, but she had other options. She snapped out a hand and sent a blast of force magic at his stomach, catching him before he could get into range to punch her again. It compromised his momentum, giving her time to throw another at his chest and a third at his head. He reeled back as his nose broke but didn't look as dazed as she would've hoped. *Dammit, this nonlethal stuff is for the birds.* She pushed thoughts of going for her throwing knives or pistol aside and dispatched a repeat trio of force blasts at her foe. The Kilomea fell without attacking again before he went down. *I need something better for these situations. Put it on the list.*

The inventory of tools and gadgets she needed to do the defender thing properly grew exponentially with each outing. She didn't see a way she'd ever catch up to it, even with help from Margrave and Kayleigh. Her attention snapped back into the moment as the next nearest foe broke into a run away from her, passing a pair of large plastic buttons mounted on the wall. Ruby dashed forward and slammed her palm against the green one, then turned to look for another opponent as the garage door started its creaking rise.

Morrigan's daggers filled her hands a moment after landing, both coated with magic to prevent anything more damaging than shallow cuts. She was skilled with them, so good that her Oriceran trainer had once described her as surgical. Her mind held no doubt that she could use them without killing.

A pair of elves appeared as she stepped through the smoke. They'd approached under cover of their illusions before abandoning them to coordinate their attacks. They were both tall, both blond, and wore identical haughty looks that she found decidedly inappropriate given the pain they were about to be in. The enemy on her right launched a blast of electricity, and she spun away from him to avoid it.

The move put her directly in the path of the second, and the level of smugness filling his face dramatically increased as he dispatched a cone of flames at her head. His expression changed to shock as the magical deflector she wore around her neck consumed the incoming power without making the telltale cracking sound that would indicate its defense had been exhausted.

His look switched from surprise to misery as she skipped forward and drove her daggers into his chest six times in rapid succession. They landed as fast as the quick jabs from a professional boxer, causing him to double over reflexively to protect the wounds. She stepped in and whipped an elbow into his temple that laid him out on the floor. A second electrical attack demolished her deflector, and the excess power sent pain along her nerves.

She ignored the sensation and threw a dagger at the other elf's face, forcing him to abandon the offensive to block. She surged forward and snapped a right cross at his head, which he stopped handily. The move twisted him to one side, allowing her left dagger to slam into his undefended side three times before he stumbled out of range. The cuts weren't deep enough to reach anything important, but the pain and blood loss would weaken him over time.

He closed with an enraged growl, wrapping his right fist in crackling magic and using his left to send shadow bolts at her. She summoned a force shield on her right hand to intercept the ranged attacks, releasing it when he punched with the magical one to grab his wrist above the lightning shield, yank his arm straight, and stab the dagger in her left fist into his triceps. He squealed in pain as she pulled on the limb again and circled the knife to stab him in the bicep as well.

A wrench of the embedded blade damaged the muscle enough that he wouldn't be able to use his arm without significant healing, and she took advantage of the injury to land a pair of punches to his head. When he tried to block her with his other arm, she slammed the hilt of her dagger into his temple. He dropped, unconscious before he hit the concrete. She reached out with force magic and yanked her thrown weapon back to her fist, then turned to find the next threat.

Idryll stalked the third Kilomea, leaping quietly over crates and sliding under the truck as he focused his attention on Morrigan. She watched the young Mist Elf's fight with her pair of enemies with one eye as she closed with the hulking giant. She respected Kilomea as a species but had none for this crew, who seemed to have tossed aside all notions of honor. *Or perhaps their loyalty is misplaced. Either way, they can't be allowed to continue threatening the police, innocent people, or my friends.* At the perfect moment, she extended her claws and slashed at the back of his ankles, intending to rip out his tendons and drive him to the floor.

She growled in frustration as he took a sudden stutter step, taking him far enough away that her attack was rebuffed by the heavy leather of his boots, failing to draw even the tiniest drop of blood. He turned as she emerged and rose to her feet, and she circled to keep him moving to defend against her. She threw punches, lulling him into expecting more, then snapped out a kick. He blocked it with a smile, seemingly unperturbed by her or her efforts. He rumbled, "You pretend to be a predator, but you're more like a house cat. Come here, kitty kitty, let me break your neck. I promise it'll be quick."

Idryll snorted. *If only you knew the truth.* Here, among the police, shifting into her tiger form was out of the question. She waited until he was in mid-step and launched herself up into the air, using her deceptively powerful leg muscles to surmount his height easily. A knee pistoned out at his head, causing him to yank it backward. His skull slammed off the side of the truck with a resounding *clang*, as she'd hoped. She grabbed the vehicle's top edge and kicked off, then whipped her legs in at his head.

He ducked, leaving her kicking metal, and she back-flipped off the vehicle to avoid his quick two-handed slam. When she landed they circled again, but now he was both angry and woozy, to judge by his expression and movements. He threw out a series of fast, hard punches, and it was her turn to block them with ease and a smile. "Is that the best you can do, big man? I have to say that I'm not impressed."

He didn't fully rise to the bait, only took a single step forward, but that was sufficient. She pivoted and slammed a sidekick down into his knee, breaking the joint. He fell to the floor, and she kicked him once more in the head, not hard enough to kill or even render him unconscious, but hopefully adequate to make sure he saw double if he decided to rejoin the fight. She headed for Morrigan's position, knowing Ruby would want her to and looked for more people to take down along the way.

Ruby dispatched another pair of dwarves with her last lightning grenade, shutting down the barrage of shadow bolts they'd been harassing her with, then launched herself back up to the rafters in response to the remaining criminals' sudden surrender. From above, she watched a flood of police and sheriff's personnel enter the warehouse in a flurry of threats and warnings. She covered Idryll in illusion and tracked both the shapeshifter and her sister as they made their retreats to the safety of the high ground.

A drone buzzed in suddenly, loud, annoying, and bigger

than those the local police used. She recognized it as a Paranormal Defense Agency bot and focused on strengthening the veils that protected her and her teammates. *I wonder if that thing can detect magic. That would be pretty useful in a lot of situations. I wouldn't put it past them to do it or at least be working on it. Add asking Margrave and Kayleigh about that possibility to the list.*

She crouched in silence as the police did their cleanup, then connected with Sheriff Alejo when she was free and away from others. "Did you invite the PDA?"

The other woman snorted. "Of course not. I told you, they're increasing their presence day by day. It's as if they know something paranormal is going on in Magic City." The sarcastic edge in her tone made Ruby laugh.

"Well, can't argue with them on that one. Although maybe they ought to be looking at the bad guys instead of focusing on the good ones."

She saw Alejo's shrug from a distance as the woman stepped through the open garage door and left the building. "I doubt we can count on them to know the difference. They think they have it all figured out, and they're not likely to look any further than that. Or to accept any new information that doesn't agree."

Ruby nodded, even though the other woman couldn't see her. "No argument. So, are we good?"

Alejo replied, "Some broken bones, a bunch of cuts that'll probably need some stitches, but certainly nothing I feel compelled to investigate. Good job, and thanks for the help."

"Nice working with you, Sheriff. Let's do it again sometime." Alejo's rueful chuckle was the other woman's only answer, and Ruby killed the connection. "All right, you two, time to get out of here. I wonder if the diner is open. Smacking down scumbags makes me hungry."

CHAPTER THREE

A giant yawn overtook Ruby as she stepped through the door to the basement lab, stopping her in her tracks and forcing her to hold onto the wall for support. *Damn. I should've slept in longer. Stupid cat.* Idryll had decided to shift to tiger-woman form halfway through the night, taking up far more space than her house cat shape did. It had already been a short night since the diner had indeed been open.

Laughter sounded from farther in the room. "Late night? Should I check to make sure Demetrius is still functioning?"

She pushed a smile onto her face, which was fairly easy, given that she actively liked her roommate and lab partner, Daphne. "Demetrius is fine. I wasn't with him yesterday. Just a late night."

"Woooo. When were you last *with* him? Come on. I want all the gory details."

Ruby's grin widened as she shook her head and crossed the room to her half of the lab. Open flames and old-school lamps lit the basement space, and it had stone walls around the long, old wood table that ran down the center and gleamed from polish and use. The witch didn't quite glow, but she radiated a sort of energy. She wore her typical flannel and jeans, with her black hair in a topknot instead of a ponytail today. "Shut it. What is this, high school?"

"Hey, some things are eternal."

Ruby shrugged the duffel bag off her shoulder and onto the table, where it landed with a *thud*. She sat and rubbed her eyes, struggling to suppress another yawn. *I wonder what a daily dose of energy potion would do to my tolerance for the stuff.* As far as she knew, no one in her circle had tried such a thing. *Maybe because they're smart enough to get sufficient sleep.* She unzipped the bag and pulled out its contents, setting a pair of medium-sized boxes on the surface beside it.

Daphne asked, "What are those?"

"These are drones, picked up from the Target south of town. It was the only store in the area open twenty-four hours that also carries technical gear. According to the Internet, they're very good. Not the best, but Margrave taught me early on not to prototype with the most expensive equipment, given how often things go catastrophically wrong."

The witch nodded and set aside the wand she'd been polishing. She rose and collected her cauldron and the portable gas burner to heat it, putting them on the table in front of her chair before sitting again. "I hear that. Plus, the more useful the thing you're creating, the more expensive the experimentation."

"Yep, exactly." Ruby took the first kit out of its box,

arraying the drone, a couple of spare parts, and the controller unit within easy reach. "What are you working on?"

"Energy potions. I think there should be a way to give them more kick and thus reduce how much you have to drink. Hopefully, the pivot point is good enough that the new formula will be profitable." She reached into the purse on the floor beside her and pulled out a vial filled with a brilliant blue liquid. "Just this was two weeks' wages. It's ridiculous."

Ruby frowned. "You need a better supplier. I can look into that for you. In the meantime, here." She pulled her key ring out of her bag, detached one of the two little metal flasks attached to it, and slid the container over. "This is a quarter dose. I keep it for, uh, in case someone in my family needs it. I have a healing one on here too if you want it."

Daphne shook her head and looked dubiously at the vial. "I don't need healing. And I'm not in a place to pay for even that much right now." Ruby could tell it cost her to admit that.

"The way I see it, we're friends, lab buddies, and who knows, maybe future business partners. Call it a loan. You can pay me back in kind when you get your new formula going. If it doesn't work out, it's not a huge loss. I'll siphon some more from my parents."

"Done deal." The other woman smiled as she snagged the vial. "So what is it you're hoping to do with that toy?"

"Margrave and I have been discussing how useful it would be to have a reconnaissance device that could detect things outside the visual and aural spectra. You know, for the police, or whatever." She tossed off the clarification nonchalantly. "Could be a moneymaker if we get it done. We're planning to upgrade the sensor array, which is pitiful at the moment, only a camera and recorder, and add in something to deliver a payload. A small one, obviously."

Ruby lifted the drone, which fit in her hand with a little overlap, to peer at it more closely. When the rotors swiveled out into flight position, the device would be about twice that size. She'd chosen that model in particular for its compact carrying form. She hadn't told Daphne any lies, as such. She and Margrave *had* discussed it, and it *would* be good for law enforcement if they ever finalized the design. However, the prototype was for her personal use, for things like scouting out enemy locations before entering them. *Or possibly security companies.*

She pulled a toolkit about the size of a briefcase off the open shelves behind her and set it on the table. Inside, each item nestled in its foam cutout, the organization and precision of the arrangement instantly soothing. She selected a thin screwdriver with the appropriate tip and started removing the plates that covered the drone's innards. "Weight will be a challenge that needs attention since the plan is to add stuff. Margrave has a 3D printer, and we're going to try plastic first, but a web of filaments rather than solid pieces like these. Hopefully that'll be enough of a reduction to compensate."

They worked in silence for several minutes. She continued her disassembly, and Daphne added ingredients to her cauldron, including a portion of the energy potion. The witch asked, "So, will the drone be part of the defenses you're putting around the house?"

Ruby nodded. "Kind of. I already have a set of techno-magical sensors out there that can run on their own for a month before needing recharging. So, if anything comes within a certain distance that's bigger than a small dog, we'll know. In addition, cameras are looking in all directions, and Demetrius programmed an algorithm to alert him if they spot things we should be concerned about."

Daphne lifted an eyebrow. "You're not going to incinerate the Amazon delivery guy by accident, are you?"

Ruby made an obscene gesture at the other woman, eliciting a laugh. "No. There are no aggressive defenses outside, only detection. However, I do have about half of the entrances set up with force shields that anyone with magic can activate. I'll have the rest covered by the end of the week or so. That would give any of you enough time to protect themselves and portal away. Plus, Shiannor suggested we might want some weapons of the mundane variety. So I'll see about making that happen, too."

"I've never fired a gun."

Ruby shrugged. "It's not hard. I'll take you to the range sometime. I'm sure your magic would provide better options, anyway."

Daphne didn't look convinced. "So, how does the drone fit into the picture?"

"Well, once we've got the prototype working, I figure we'll modify some bigger ones with the improved sensors, plus video and audio tied into Demetrius' surveillance bot. Then it's a matter of keeping them up in rotation." She didn't mention the magical cloak of illusion to conceal it from visual detection that she planned to include if she could work out how to do it.

The witch snorted. "So, we'll be the only house on the block with twenty-four-seven aerial surveillance? That'll be subtle."

Ruby laughed. "I'll paint them blue so they look like the sky. I could even add clouds. Will that help? And you can't have it both ways. You want protection. I'm giving you protection."

Again, they worked in silence until Daphne cursed. "Damn. I found another one that didn't work."

"How do you know?"

"It went inert. Turned brown. Somehow the magics canceled each other."

"Well, consider it an investment in narrowing things down, right?"

"Yeah." She flicked off the burner and pulled out a notebook, scribbling quickly. "That's all I have time for today. I need to find some food and get to work at the Ebon Dragon. Honestly, the mental shifts from the day job to trying to do this stuff are as damaging as the lost time."

"Do you have some vacation coming up or something? I could make sure nobody bothers you."

Daphne shook her head. "None for nine months, unfortunately. Still, the trip to Mexico to see the Mayan ruins was totally worth it, so I guess I can't complain." Her face told a different story as she finished cleaning her area.

Liam stepped through the door with a wave. "Morning, ladies." The dwarf was bright and bubbly, his blond hair free this morning, his beard lacking its regular braids.

They greeted him, and Ruby asked, "What's up?"

He shrugged. "Heading over to the Grinding Axes for a

bite and a beer. You both should come with. Mick and Jas are probably missing you."

The other woman glanced down at her watch and nodded. "If we make it fast, I can do it."

He applauded the decision with eager clapping, then looked at Ruby. "Excellent, and you?"

She shook her head. "I'm up to my elbows in drone guts. I need to get this finished or Margrave will kill me."

"Well, when you've finished, drop by. I'm off today, so I might stick around, help serve some drinks, that sort of thing."

Ruby grinned. "You got it." Inside, though, she knew her day would hold no such recreational opportunities. *Work, work, work. I hope she figures out the improved energy potion. Maybe I could use it in place of sleep and get caught up on stuff.*

CHAPTER FOUR

Ruby had indulged in a luxurious shower at her parents' house as soon as she arrived, having given up on the drones in a momentary fit of frustration. The bathing facilities at the home she shared with her roommates on the surface couldn't compete with the one in the kemana. *Magic for the win, at least in maintaining perfectly hot water.* She dressed in sweatpants and a sweatshirt, planning to sleep over, and headed down to dinner, patting Idryll in passing. *Mental note, get the tiger some food so she doesn't chew my arm off.*

She was the next-to-last to arrive, darting through the doorway ahead of her sister, who gave her a gentle smack on the back of the head in response. Ruby laughed. "Slowpoke."

"Yeah, whatever. I was busy with work. That thing that responsible people do. Perhaps you've heard of it?"

She slid into her seat beside her brother Dralen, who observed, "I'm pretty sure she doesn't understand anything about it. She went off to college and came back a slacker."

Ruby ferociously scowled as she plopped her napkin into her lap. "I'm an innovator, I'll have you know. An entrepreneur, even. Genius takes time." She lifted her chin on the last line in case anyone missed her theatrical arrogance.

Morrigan replied, "Oh, right, I forgot. It's not lying around all day. It's *seeking inspiration.*"

Their mother, Sinnia Achera, sighed loudly. "Okay, enough of that." The chef delivered dinner, a vegetable casserole large enough to feed all of them, and a pan of lasagna that was even bigger. Ruby snagged the Italian dish and stabbed out a chunk for herself before anyone could get at it. Dralen tried to reach for it and received a slap on the hand for his trouble. When she'd grabbed another half-portion, she passed it to him. Her brother served himself, then twisted to look at their father, Rayar Achera, in his customary seat at the head of the table. "So, did you hear?"

He nodded. He'd chosen a new hairstyle, clipped short so the grey was less noticeable than the white, and it made his sharp features seem even more so. "I did. It turned out about as well as you could expect. Which is to say, not well at all."

Ruby asked, "A little more information for those who aren't up to speed?"

Morrigan muttered, "You can say that again," and Ruby kicked her.

The edges of her father's lips turned down. "The message went out to Gabriel Sloane that no more casinos can be built because of a new zoning restriction. From now on, they're only allowed on the Strip and only to the current boundaries. He was not pleased, to say the least."

Sinnia replied, "Understatement of the year. I heard from Jailynne that Sloane destroyed the hotel room he'd rented for the meeting and that the representative basically ran for his life."

Ruby bobbed her head. "That would constitute not taking it well, I guess. So, is that problem settled?"

Dralen snorted. "With a man like The Nightmare? Somehow I doubt it." Ruby agreed, and the nods from the others at the table showed that they did, too.

She asked, "Anything we should do?"

Rayar replied, "We all need to keep an eye out for anything unusual. For you in particular, Ruby, there might be more. We'll talk about it after dinner." That decisively shut the door on further discussion of the matter, and they enjoyed the meal, filling it with laughter and companionship. She'd missed that feeling a lot while she was away. Sure, she could have portaled back at any time, but she'd wanted to have the real college experience. *Whatever that is. Pretending to be human at school when you're a magical from another planet probably isn't it, though.*

After a dessert of fresh berries and whipped cream topped with a drizzle of honey, she followed her father into his study. He sat behind the desk, rather than in the chairs by the fire, which told her this would probably be a conversation involving business at their casino, Spirits. However, the delivery of two tumblers of whiskey shortly after that indicated it didn't rise to the level of an emergency and that she wasn't in trouble—presumably. Her dad possessed rarely used master-grade skills in misdirection.

He leaned back in his chair and sipped the whiskey before setting the glass on the desk. His voice was level and businesslike. "It's time, Ruby. You can keep innovating and entrepreneuring in your off-hours, but we need you at Spirits. These are tumultuous times, and you have brains and a unique perspective we can use. We'll give you any job you like, from roving consultant down to division manager, if you want it. Eventually, you'll have to spend some time working in each area the way that your brother and sister are so that you know how to do everything, but that can come later."

Ruby sighed and took a deep drink of her beverage before setting it on the desk. She leaned forward and looked her father in the eyes. "Dad, I can't. I'd like to, but I have other things to do. Before you ask, they're important, and I have no way of knowing if they're more or less important than helping out with Spirits. Still, I know you have good people there, and I think there are tasks here in Ely that only I can handle."

He frowned but didn't otherwise show his displeasure. "What kind of tasks?"

"I've recently been able to remember more about my *venamisha*. The tests gave big hints, really obvious ones, that I'm supposed to figure out what's going on here in Magic City."

"An Oriceran ritual told you to do things on Earth?"

She sighed and released a low chuckle. "There's the famous family debater we all know and love bringing pointed logic into play. No, it didn't mention Ely by name, but it was clear. My people on Oriceran don't need help at the moment. My people here do."

He nodded and delayed his next response with another sip of the alcohol. She matched him, enjoying the burn as it slipped down her throat. He asked, "Why you? You're not an investigator or anything. No offense, but usually specialists train to do this sort of thing."

"I've asked myself the same question." *Because I've named myself the city's defender, that's why. Damn, I wish I could tell you that. However, secrecy is safety.* "I'm smart, I know the town from before, and I'm learning the way it is now. That gives me a different perspective than anyone who hasn't been away. Plus, Sheriff Alejo is beginning to trust me, even if the Paranormal Defense Agency is too paranoid to." She laughed. "*Paranoid* defense agency, more like."

He lifted his glass in a false toast. "To that bunch of idiots, may they soon leave our town." He finished his whiskey. "What you're doing sounds dangerous."

"No more so than for anyone else in Ely at the moment. No one signs on to be casino staff with the expectation that they'll be facing armed intruders on a regular basis."

"Touché." He sighed. "We'll put a pin in this conversation, but it's not over. Ultimately, you need to be with us at Spirits."

She nodded. "I know, Dad. Believe me. I'm keenly aware of all my obligations. I have to stack them one after the other instead of all at the same time. Speaking of time pressure, I have a friend with an interesting idea." She explained Daphne's plan to improve energy potions, as well as some other things the witch had been working on. "I think if we could put her on the payroll at the casino for a month as a trial, let's say, she might come up with something good. Consider it an investment. We can give her the freedom she needs to work on this in exchange for a percentage of what results."

He tapped a finger against his teeth, something only he did when he was seriously thinking. "This her idea?"

"No, mine. She mentioned not having enough time, that's all. You know me, I'm always looking for ways to bring magic and business together."

He gave a decisive nod. "Okay. We can do that. Since she won't be doing casino stuff, there shouldn't be a problem with the Ebon Dragon's owners. She'll have to inform them, nonetheless. Can't have any suspicion of underhandedness, not at this moment."

"Understood."

Ruby had risen to head to the kitchen and retrieve some food for Idryll when he said, "On one condition."

She settled back in the chair with a sigh. "Of course." She grinned at her father. "What is it?"

"You spend an eight-hour day each week working at Spirits, learning the positions. You'll do it while she's on the payroll, a month, a year, however long it turns out to be."

She nodded. "You're awfully good at what you do, Dad. Deal, but only if I get a percentage personally of whatever she brings to the company since I'm putting in sweat equity."

Her father laughed. "You're not bad at what you do either, Ruby. Done."

CHAPTER FIVE

Ruby looked around in dismay at the contents of all the bags she'd dumped onto her bedroom floor. "You know, this trying to operate out of two houses and stuffing things in bags and throwing bags through portals and forgetting about the bags is not a productive way to live."

From the bed at her back, Morrigan replied, "Unlike how the rest of your life runs at such a high level of productivity, you mean."

"Shut it. Ow," she griped as she stubbed her toe on her spell-casting dagger.

Another laugh came from behind her, this time from Idryll, who lay beside her sister. *Apparently, I'm great entertainment today.* "You should let me come along with you. I can help you stay organized, for one thing."

Ruby bent, snagged the dagger, and tossed it into the backpack she planned to take with her to Oriceran. "First, you're not exactly the height of organization either. It's not like you own things you need to keep tabs on. Second, shut up." She shook her head and knelt, lifting her equipment belt with its techno-magical gadgets. "I suppose these might work properly over there, but it's equally possible that they'd go wrong and I'd wind up stunning myself or something. Best if I leave them."

Idryll reiterated, "Which is another reason you should take me with you."

Ruby sighed and ran her hands through her hair to get it out of her eyes and turned to face the others. "Repeating the request over and over isn't going to make it happen. I've thought about it a lot, believe me. If everything else were equal, I would love nothing more than to have you with me to soak up whatever injuries might occur." The cat stuck her tongue out, and Ruby gave her the same in return. "However, I have this strong feeling that if I bring anyone with magic other than the normal Mist Elf kind, it could be a problem."

Idryll replied dryly, "So, you're a mystic now?"

Morrigan added, "Can I have your stuff when you move into the monastery or whatever?"

"No to both of you. Besides, it's not like you'll be bored. While I'm away, you need to keep an eye on things around here, make sure there's no major trouble headed in our direction."

Her sister looked at the tiger-woman. "Maybe we should wrap this whole thing up before she gets back. What do you think?"

Idryll nodded. "An excellent plan. I bet we could do it, too. We break into the security company and kill both of the owners. Problem solved."

Ruby snorted. "First, if you're stupid enough to imagine our problems begin and end with those chuckleheads, you're way dumber than I believe you are. That's a pretty high bar for both of you to overcome. Second, no, we're not randomly killing people."

Morrigan sighed. "Always with the excuses."

Idryll replied, "I know, right?"

Her sister said, "Okay, but seriously, we should at least make some progress while watching for trouble. What do you think is our best approach?"

Ruby shrugged. "I'd say the most likely place to get new and useful information is the black-market ring. It seems as if that's connected to all sorts of garbage here in town. So, there could be some people we can lean on, the way Alejo did with that informant." *It's not like I'm going to be able to stop you from doing something anyway, so it might as well be something productive.*

Morrigan replied, "That makes sense to me. How about you?" She turned her head to look at Idryll.

"Sure. I still think targets of opportunity need to be viewed as opportunities, not ignored because of some antiquated moral code."

Ruby pointed a finger. "No killing unless your life is in danger." Her partner opened her mouth to speak, and she added loudly to stop her, "I mean *imminent* peril. Not some sort of ambient, existential, 'our lives are all in jeopardy all the time' kind of thing."

The pair on the bed laughed and nodded agreement, albeit reluctantly in the tiger-woman's case. Ruby continued, "If you find something, tell Demetrius, and he can get it to Alejo anonymously. I'll talk to him about it before I leave. Now, I'm in a hurry, so shut up. I need to get this stuff together."

Morrigan teased, "Oh, you're pressed for time, but you still have enough to go see Demetrius, is that it?"

She laughed and ignored the heat she felt rising in her ears. "Well, I do have to say goodbye. You know, it's possible I won't come back."

Her sister snorted. "One of those 'take me one last time before I go into battle' kind of things? Pretty stereotypical, sis."

Ruby decided she had enough flex in her schedule to pummel her furiously with a pillow, so she did.

She arrived in her family's house on Oriceran with a backpack carrying her essential items over one shoulder and her sheathed sword in the other hand. A noise from her bedroom revealed that her mentor was waiting, as she'd promised. Ruby headed into that chamber and found Keshalla sitting on the room's only chair. Beside her on a small table was a bundle wrapped in red paper. Ruby asked, "What is that?"

Keshalla shook her head. "Always looking for shortcuts," she imitated Idryll. "Open it and see."

Ruby picked up the object, which was heavier than expected. Opening the package revealed a pair of supple leather garments in the brilliant blue and silver that were her house colors. "Are we going somewhere fancy?"

Her teacher chuckled. "I'd say questing for an artifact weapon is pretty fancy. Besides, you've completed two *venamishas*. You're someone of status now, whether you want to be or not. You should dress the part."

Ruby ran her hands over the supple material. "Will it be as protective as my current gear? It seems thinner."

"It will, and it is. Plus, it's lighter, so you'll be able to move faster, hopefully."

"Yeah, yeah, I know. I need to practice using magic to speed up my movements."

Her teacher nodded. "You do." She rose, and Ruby realized she wasn't in her standard armor, either. This outfit was black and red like the other one, but this was fancier, featuring hand-tooled designs covering almost all of it. She wore knives at her hips, a pair of swords across her back, and doubtless had daggers hidden in her boots.

Ruby said, "Well, you've clearly upped the sartorial ante. I guess I don't have a choice."

She donned the new clothes, which fit her perfectly and did indeed restrict her far less than either her training outfit on Oriceran or her fighting gear on Earth did. She remarked, "Wow. This is nice. Thank you. I don't suppose I can get a set to use on the other planet?"

Keshalla laughed. "What, one gift isn't enough?" When Ruby tried to protest, her mentor raised a hand. "I anticipated your request. It's being worked on now and should be ready for you by the time we finish with this, assuming it doesn't take a week or anything."

"How long do you think it'll be?"

The other woman shrugged. "Logically, I would say less than a day, but that's a guess. Where magic is involved, time can move differently. I don't think we'll be trapped under the mountain for a decade or anything if that's what you're worried about."

Ruby rolled her eyes. "How reassuring. You're filling me

with hope for this endeavor." She added the rest of her gear in silence. First on was the belt with the dagger sheath at her left hip. Then, the bandolier to hold her sword properly positioned for a draw from behind her right shoulder. Finally, her throwing knives that Shentia had provided went into custom holders in her boots, with no telltale sticking out to betray their presence. The weapons' ability to pierce magical defenses had been the key to defeating Goryo the first time she'd faced him, and she felt far more confident with the blades than without them. *I'll need every bit of confidence I can get to head into that mountain again.*

She drew a deep breath to center herself. "How do I look?"

Keshalla replied, "Wonderful. Fantastic. Drop-dead gorgeous. If your fighting skills matched the quality of your appearance, I wouldn't have to come along, probably."

"But you're going to."

"Of course. If you're defeated, someone needs to take the sword as their own."

Ruby squeezed her hands into fists and released the tension, warming them up. "Are you sure it's a sword?"

Her teacher shrugged. "Everything seems to point that way, although you know, the description is indirect, at best."

"Does the prophecy that mentions this give us any other good information?"

Keshalla shook her head. "Only that danger awaits and you're probably the right one to face it."

She barked a laugh. "I don't like the sound of that 'probably.'"

"That's the best that the mystics have to offer, it seems."

Ruby sighed. "Okay, do we know where to start, at least?"

Keshalla nodded. "The entrance is about halfway down the mountain from where we are now."

"Well, we don't have to climb up the damn rock. Things are already looking up. Let's do this."

CHAPTER SIX

Morrigan and Idryll had reached the surface through Spirits, using illusion to hide their costumes from prying eyes and the omnipresent security cameras. They quickly crossed the pedestrian strip and passed through the towering casino complexes on the opposite side, then made their way to the rooftops of the town beyond.

Morrigan said, "Ruby's right about one thing. It would be a lot more convenient to have a place where we could safely gear up on the surface, rather than relying on an illusion that might be noticed if the magic failed."

Idryll shrugged. "That would seem to be something you two could manage, given a little effort. It's not as if your family lacks resources."

"Problem is, while my folks have a lot, they watch over it *very* carefully. I'd guess we have less monetary freedom than most people our age since our personal accounts are wrapped up in the business. Tax purposes, or whatever. I don't claim to understand it. Dralen probably does."

"So, what prey do you wish to hunt tonight?"

Morrigan chuckled. "Well, we need to pursue the black-market ring to make Ruby happy. However, it seems to me that Grentham is part of that, in addition to being one of the owners of Aces Security. So, finding him and following him would be honoring the promise we made to focus on the black market, right?"

The shapeshifter laughed. "You're sneakier than your sister. I like that."

"Smarter, too. I coincidentally asked Demetrius where our target is known to hang out, figuring Ruby was having him watched. She was, and he usually starts his evenings at the Double Down. How about we go take a look?"

"Perfect. I'll lead." Idryll headed for the roof edge and jumped across the narrow alley separating their building from the next. Morrigan ran in pursuit and made the jump without using her magic. They continued that way, rooftop to rooftop until they reached one opposite the club. The shapeshifter asked, "Shall we go in under an illusion?"

"I think we have a better option." She handed over a black plastic box, about the size of a deck of cards but notably heavier than it looked. "Can you get this on the roof over there without being seen? It needs to be as near the center as possible."

Idryll snorted. "Please, you have to ask?" Morrigan cloaked the shapeshifter in a veil just in case, but her stealthy passage likely wouldn't be noticed, given her skills. She descended to the street, crossed, and climbed up the side of the building hidden in the shadows filling the alley beside it. When Idryll returned, Morrigan activated the connection to Demetrius. "Hey, D, your hack box is in place."

The infomancer's annoyed voice replied, "Quit calling it a hack box. It's a signal booster."

"Yep. Like I said. Hack box."

He sighed. "You know, I don't have to help you."

Morrigan answered sweetly, "You mean because we're not sleeping together like you and my sister? We can change that, big boy." She put all the sarcastic lasciviousness into the comment that she could, and he laughed.

"First of all, I'd never do that to Ruby. Second of all, you're not my type."

"Not into the brainy ones, is that it? Pretty and dumb is your thing?"

He heaved a sigh and decided he'd lost the battle or at least wasn't interested in continuing to fight it. "Okay, I'm into the club's cameras. Pathetic defenses. I'm looking for Grentham?"

"You got it. We only need to know if he's in there."

"Yep, I've spotted him. Table in the back, surrounded by dwarves, probably flunkies based on their body language."

Morrigan grinned. "Perfect. Tell us when he moves?"

"Sure. You'll handle submitting my bill to Spirits?"

"Of course. Since we don't share a *personal* relationship like you and my sister, we'll have to do it with money." She heard the beginning of another exasperated sigh before he turned off the connection. She laughed. "Too easy."

It took forty-five minutes before their target exited, and they followed him from above as he walked down the street toward the nearest of his pawnshops. She'd wondered before why he didn't portal to the place. Ruby's opinion was that he liked being seen, enjoyed being perceived as a man of the people, as part of the community. In any case, it made tracking him possible. Morrigan and Ruby agreed it wasn't a long-term solution, though. They needed a better way to keep tabs on targets in general and follow them if they chose to use magical transport. Her sister claimed she was working on it, but Morrigan planned to bring it up with Margrave herself, nonetheless.

She carried a burner phone and recorded pictures and videos of the various shops he stopped in to share with Alejo. He visited three before suddenly entering a small specialty shop they'd never connected him to before. It wasn't a pawnshop, but it did sell magic items. Morrigan said, "I wonder if this is the legitimate face of the operation or something? Maybe money-laundering, like on TV shows?"

Idryll shrugged. "I don't think I've seen those shows. It would be good to know what's going on inside there. Will your fancy box work?"

Morrigan shook her head. "There won't be cameras in there, I'm sure. Criminals tend not to enjoy being watched and recorded. We'll need to do it the hard way." They descended to street-level, crossed to the opposite side, and searched all accessible surfaces of the cube, including the roof. The structure had no windows, and only two doors, neither of which would be easy or quiet to open. She growled, "Dammit. I guess we go back up and wait until he comes out. Hopefully, there's nothing super important going on in there."

Goryo had silently observed the dwarf's entrance from a hidden corner inside, pleased to see he had come alone. While he could have simply destroyed the place to find what he was looking for, he preferred finesse whenever possible. When he'd put the word out on the streets about the presence of the precious object contained in the shop, he'd been sure it would generate a response. As always, it was nice to be right.

He said, "Good of you to come."

Grentham spun with his hands raised, ready to defend or attack, and Goryo made a clucking noise over the pistol he held pointed at the other man's face. "Remain calm. It's loaded with anti-magic rounds. There's no need for us to fight. We are, more or less, on the same side."

His response was a snarled, "I would say less than more on that front."

Goryo inclined his head. "As you wish. Nonetheless, I believe our mutual employer made it clear you are to provide me with whatever tools I require, correct?"

Grentham sighed. "Yeah, he did. So, I presume you've been through the place?"

"No. I chose to wait so you could show me around." The grinding of the other man's teeth was audible, and he inwardly smiled while maintaining a stoic expression. The dwarf dropped his hands, and he lowered the weapon. "Shall we?"

His unwilling host showed him the various objects in the cabinets, which included weapons and defenses, plus pendants and spelled jewelry of multiple kinds. The only thing they all had in common was their potency, which was higher than items sold in the city's other shops. Goryo observed, "I had wondered where the best pieces were held. Now I know. Who are your clients?"

"Mr. and Mrs. None-of-your-business, buddy."

Goryo laughed. "I understand it's hard to know your employer has so little faith in you that he felt the need to bring me in. Don't worry. My time here is transitional. Once the very lucrative contract I've undertaken is complete, you won't see me again. So, ultimately, it's in your best interest to assist me." He pointed at several objects. "I'll take those."

Grentham sighed but collected them and handed them over, each in its soft fabric bag. "See that you return those when you finish with the task. Nothing about the arrangement said you get to keep my stuff."

Goryo nodded. "Except for one item."

"Which one?"

"The one you haven't shown me. The one you have hidden away in a secure location. The most valuable object in the shop. You know of what I speak."

Grentham growled, "How did you find out about that?"

He shrugged. "I have my ways. Now, give it to me." He twitched the pistol slightly to emphasize his command.

For a moment, he thought the dwarf would balk, would decide that battle was preferable to surrendering the precious object. However, the other man turned, grumbled, and walked into the back room. Goryo followed at a careful distance and watched him spin the dial on a large combination lock, then open the door of the heavy safe. Grentham placed an ornate black carved wooden box on the table on the desk. "There. Go ahead and put it on."

Goryo shook his head. "I am neither stupid nor uninformed, dwarf. Open the container." With a sigh, as if to say that his patience had reached its end, the other man removed the top to reveal a silver octopus-shaped bracelet, large enough to go over wrist and forearm. "Good. Now close the box and step away."

Grentham grinned as he did so. "Sure you don't want to put it on here?"

Goryo stared hard into the other man's eyes. "I'm aware of the bonding process, which would make that decidedly dangerous, even if I was able to trust your motives fully."

"Well, I guess you can't give that one back, at least not voluntarily."

Goryo stepped forward and took the box, then backed out toward the front door. "Indeed. Thank you for your obedience." He turned and left, moving quickly to enter an autonomous vehicle he had arranged earlier. Within moments, he was blocks away.

Grentham yelled a string of curses at sufficient volume that he was sure people heard him halfway down the block. When he'd gotten himself under control, he pulled out his phone and called his partner. "Our friend visited to get some supplies. He's in the wind. I think any obligation we had to him, other than finding him and killing him when all this is over, is done."

Jared Trenton replied, "Good. We'll start thinking about

how to do that right after we figure out the plan to take out those costumed bastards who have been getting in the way of our operations. That's a conversation for tomorrow, at the office. For now, meet at The Armory, half an hour?"

Grentham sighed. "Yeah, I could use a drink. See you there."

CHAPTER SEVEN

The entry into the mountain was uneventful, and the path beyond led downward in a gentle spiral. The passage was narrow, the ceiling only a foot higher than Ruby's head, and offered a pronounced feeling of claustrophobia with rough-hewn walls less than an arm's reach away to the left and right. After an hour of walking, they arrived at what appeared to be a resting place, an area carved into the outer side of the passageway suitably large for three or four people to relax in comfort. They agreed to forge on, both eager to get to the task ahead.

When they came to the next opportunity to step off the path an hour later, Ruby was annoyed, hungry, and in need of a break from the plodding monotony of putting one foot in front of the other. She collapsed onto the floor, and her teacher laughed. "Giving up already, *minari?*

Ruby shook her head. "Not at all. Refueling for what's to come." She handed over one of several protein bars she'd brought along and tore into another.

Keshalla sat beside her and took a small bite with a grimace. "I don't know how you eat these things. We should've made some decent trail bread."

Ruby nodded. She was a big fan of the heavy, dried fruit and nut-filled provisions that were the Mist Elves' historical road food. "Yeah, but we didn't have time, so quit complaining." She drank from one of the canteens she'd brought along and shared it with her teacher. "So, what else do you know about what's coming for us?"

Keshalla lifted an eyebrow. "Technically, we are going to it, not the other way around." Ruby stuck out her tongue, and her mentor replied with an imperious nod. "In any case, no one knows much. I will share the legend if you think you can behave long enough to hear it."

She made a show of considering the question, then shrugged. "I'll do my best. No promises."

The other woman rolled her eyes and drank from the canteen before continuing. "So, once upon a time, a solitary Mist Elf locked himself away from the rest of our people with the intent of focusing purely on his magical research."

She interrupted, "I can see the appeal of that. My roommates are always distracting me when I try to work on a project."

Her teacher scowled. "Yes, isn't it annoying when you're interrupted?"

Ruby laughed. "Boom. Point for you. I'll shut up."

"Gods be praised. Anyway, it's believed he created a series of defenses to protect himself from outsiders, and when they were complete, sent a message to the nearby villages telling them to leave him alone."

She interrupted again, "But they didn't."

"You're very wise." The sarcastic tone left her teacher's voice as she continued, "In any case, yes, many did try to find him, either as a game for unwise children, a rite of passage for young adults, or possibly for more nefarious purposes on the part of the adults who made the attempt. After all, who knows what he might have created in his hermitage, right?" Ruby nodded but remained silent, earning her a nod of approval from Keshalla. "Most of the latter didn't return, and the younger ones who did make it back never tried again. As with the *venamisha*, something prevented them from being able to talk about the experience afterward, so we don't fully know."

"Magic that causes people to forget your defenses is a great plan if you want to keep them from sharing knowledge to figure out your tricks and traps. I wonder if I could get one of those for my roommates."

Keshalla ignored her comment. "In the end, a mystic had a dream about him. In it, the hermit spoke of the one who would eventually discover his secrets, and the mystics chose to believe it was a true foretelling."

"And it said?"

"I'm paraphrasing, but the vision showed the person as young, with a foot on both sides of reality, a conqueror of battles of might, wit, and wisdom, fully capable of undertaking the horrific battle that awaits those who quest for his knowledge."

Ruby scowled. "That doesn't sound particularly positive."

Keshalla shrugged. "The mystics predicted it would be someone with an unusual mental state, possibly multiple personalities. They were looking primarily for news of anyone who had returned damaged from the world in between. Now they know it's an average crazy person. Namely, you."

She replied dryly, "Ha, ha, ha. This mystic thing seems more like a dice roll than a science."

"Very possible."

Ruby was silent for a moment, then another. Finally, she asked, "Did anyone mention what kind of defenses the hermit created? Because that scraping sounds like it's getting louder." Both women climbed to their feet and peered down the passageway, but its curve prevented them from seeing anything.

Keshalla replied, "I already told you no information got out. Still, it certainly seems as if we might have discovered the outer layer of his protection." She drew her daggers, more appropriate than a sword for the corridor's confined area.

Ruby pulled out hers and summoned a force buckler on her other arm. "All right. Let's go find whoever is making that irritating noise and make them stop."

Sound traveled strangely through the structure because it was ten more minutes before the passage emerged into a chamber. It was almost shocking, after the unbroken uniformity of most of their descent, to see the large open space. It was a perfect dome, the top arcing high above, smooth walls descending to a flat surface of polished stone. A glowing ball that hovered near the uppermost point of the room provided illumination. It was empty except for what had once been a Mist Elf male but was now something more. *Or less, maybe.*

He wore only tattered trousers that left most of his body on display. It was a mixture of flesh and metal, arranged with no particular logic, almost as if the foreign substance had grown from within according to some design only it understood. The scraping came from a heavy metal chain wrapped around his torso that dragged on the floor behind him as he moved slowly through the space. His path was seemingly random, as he changed direction in fits and starts. One abrupt turn caused the chain to whip out like a weapon, whistling through the air.

Ruby said, "Okay, that's really weird, and that chain is deeply worrisome. Very dangerous. You go first."

Keshalla shook her head and traded her daggers for swords. Ruby followed suit, drawing her sword and gripping her spell dagger in her offhand. Her teacher observed, "We should come at him from different sides. One has to assume there's more than the chain if he's supposed to be an actual deterrent."

"Maybe his purpose is only to scare off potential intruders?"

"Perhaps. It would make far more sense to have him do both, and it is a magical scientist we're talking about here. Except for you, I've found all of those I've encountered to be highly logical."

Ruby nodded and let the jibe pass unanswered. "Okay. I'll go left. You go right." She moved without waiting for a response. The figure didn't react, simply kept moving as if she wasn't there. *Well, hell, this almost seems unfair.* The thought had barely crossed her mind when the ambushers struck. Large slabs of stone, previously invisible due to their perfect integration with the walls, fell inward to reveal four more flesh-and-metal figures.

The two nearest Ruby rushed her, and she had a moment to realize they each had a large, pointed spike in place of a forearm and a hand and carried a small shield in the other. The circular bucklers were etched with runes and shone in defiance of their likely age. A yelp escaped her, and she charged back the way she had come, not wanting to put herself between the chain-dragger and the other two. Her teacher did the same on the opposite side of the room.

It segmented the enemies neatly, two of the newcomers going after Keshalla, two of them rushing her. She settled her weight and positioned her sword in a diagonal guard, then thrust the dagger toward the nearest to dispatch a force bolt at him. The magic flew out, causing the air to ripple from its passage, and her foe lifted the shield to block it. The impact slowed him but didn't stop him. Ruby yelled, "The shields can absorb a portion of power cast at them."

Her teacher shouted back, "Got it. The metal parts of their bodies aren't impervious, but it would take quite a while to hack through them. Aim for the flesh."

Ruby stepped to her right to ensure the closest enemy was between her and the one she'd struck with her magic. She sent a force blast at his feet, and he reacted by leaping into the air and whipping a metal leg around at her head far faster than she expected he could. Her only defense was to collapse to the floor, and she turned the move into a foot sweep, her heel connecting with his flesh-and-bone foot to topple him. She spun up in time to catch the other man's spike on her sword, the direct impact of strength against strength sending pain through her hand and arm.

She called, "Damn, these things are strong," and stabbed her dagger through to slash at the wrist of the shield hand. He dropped it as she scored a line of blood on his flesh. She'd planned to give the one on the floor a kick to the head, but he was already spinning to try to take her legs out, and she wanted no part of ground fighting with either of the pair. A blind jump backward took her out of range, and she cringed until her boots hit the surface again.

She discharged a cone of flame large enough to encompass both of her enemies. The one she'd knocked down interposed a shield that drank some of the power and caused the rest to flow around him. The other wasn't so quick, and his organic portions blistered from the heat. He collapsed with a scream of pain, and it reminded Ruby why fire seemed almost as much a punishment as a weapon. A scrape and a whistle entered her consciousness from her right side, and she immediately fell and tumbled into a backward somersault, feeling the heavy chain catch at her hair as she moved.

Ruby rolled up and sidestepped another slash from the metal links, this one a diagonal that would've struck her at the joint of shoulder and neck. She blasted him with force, and where the magic crossed the path of the chain, the weapon soaked it in. She turned, ran toward her teacher's sole remaining opponent, and thrust her sword through him from behind before he knew she was there. "The chain absorbs magic, too."

Keshalla shook her head. "A formidable defense indeed. Why did you leave the ambusher alive?"

Ruby scowled at her. "Oh, I thought it would be more fun. Tell you what, you deal with the big guy and I'll go take the other one out." Unfortunately, Keshalla was already in motion toward the last ambusher, who had gained his feet and was rushing to engage, leaving the one with the chain for Ruby. She muttered, "Fine, be that way," then raised her voice and shouted, "Hey, ugly. Bring it on."

Her taunt had zero effect, and his progress toward her had the same fits and starts as his plodding walk. *I wonder if he's broken, or maybe whatever passes for his mind has been damaged by the monotony of wandering the room.* The chain came down at a diagonal, and she sidestepped it, then the figure circled it up and tried the same attack again. "Okay, so you have a big weapon, but you're not very bright. I get it."

She layered her left arm in force magic several inches thick and charged him with a yell. Predictably, he whipped the chain at her, and she caught the blow on her arm, letting the tip wrap around it. It buzzed as it chewed on the power that protected her, and the pain of that assault radiated through her skeleton. She grabbed the chain and yanked it, which hurt even more but pulled him a step off balance. It provided the room she needed to slip forward and drive her sword through the side of his neck that was metal-free. He fell without a sound, like a robot with its electricity cut, and blood seeped from the wound.

She sensed an approach and turned, raising her blade to block, but it was only her teacher. Ruby sighed. "Well. That was fun. Can we head home now?"

Keshalla shook her head. "You don't want to disappoint the mystics, do you?"

"Jury's out."

Her mentor laughed and pointed at one of the alcoves. "There's another passage behind that opening. Looks dangerous. You go first." Ruby sheathed her sword, pulled out her dagger, and obeyed her mentor's instruction.

CHAPTER EIGHT

The passage led downward for only a dozen or so revolutions before opening into a new room. Several feet inside the entrance lay three separate openings to different corridors. Ruby groaned. "Decisions. I hate decisions."

"That explains a lot about you."

"Yeah, yeah. How about the middle?"

"Lead on."

As soon as she stepped across the threshold, a barrier appeared behind her, sizzling into place with a burst of magic. She spun and pushed against it, receiving a shock in return. "Ow, damn hell *damn*. Force *and* lightning? Kind of overkill, if you ask me."

The magical wall didn't block sound. Keshalla replied, "Looks like we're on our own for the moment. I'll take the left one. Call out whenever you make a turn so we can keep track of each other."

She nodded. "Sorry I got you into this."

Her teacher laughed. "I got myself into this, as you might recall," and stepped out of view. Ruby called out when she made a right turn, then again when she made a left, but no reply sounded in return. She pushed worry to the back of her mind, knowing that if anyone was capable of making it through to the other end, it was Keshalla. *Probably more likely to survive this than I am, to be honest.*

The attack came out of nowhere as a panel slid aside unexpectedly to reveal another of the flesh-and-metal amalgams. This version wore only a strange faded green loincloth, thankfully in better shape than the trousers the last had worn. Both of his arms ended in the wicked spikes, and they stabbed out at her in tandem. She intercepted one with the force shield and caught the other on the dagger's crosspiece, circling the weapon out and away. She slammed a kick into his stomach, but the metal there proved to be unyielding.

The thing's only fleshy parts were one leg, the other thigh, and part of his upper arm. He snapped his forehead at her in a head butt, and she threw herself backward to avoid it. *No more broken noses, thanks.* The move left her pressed back against the wall, and he took advantage of the situation and pinned her there. She tried to wriggle out to her right, and the spike on that side slammed into the wall, blocking her way. Trying to do the same in the opposite direction met the same result.

She snapped her dagger up at his face, and he jerked his head to the side to avoid the point. It was weird seeing his body react without any change to the expression on his metallic features. She took advantage of the distraction to smash her knee into his groin. His reaction suggested the loincloth covered flesh rather than metal as his breath shot out and he staggered backward. She followed up with a slice to his upper arm and blasted flame at the living portion of his leg. He screamed in pain and threw himself bodily at her, smashing her back against the wall. Her skull cracked against the rock, sending stars through her vision, and a trickle of blood from her scalp slipped onto her neck and made her shiver.

Ruby growled, "Okay, scumbag, enough of that." She took an extra moment to gather her power and blasted it out in a force wave. Unlike the previous room's enemies, this one didn't have much capacity for magic absorption. He flew backward and crashed into the wall behind him. She threw another focused blast at his face, slamming his skull back off the rock. *You did it to me. Now I did it to you. Fair play.* The way he sank to the ground, clearly dazed, suggested living matter inside his metal skull, too. She stepped forward and kicked it, smashing his head into the stone again. He fell flat on his face and stopped moving.

Ruby reached a hand back to check her damage, and it returned covered in blood. She pulled the healing flask from her belt and drank a quarter of it, stiffening momentarily in discomfort as the wound sealed itself. She stored the vial, drew a deep breath, then continued forward, looking for her next challenge.

Keshalla stalked through the passageway, calling out each directional decision she made, not at all convinced her voice was carrying to her student. She wasn't afraid for Ruby, was confident she could handle whatever she might encounter as long as she kept her wits about her. *Hopefully, I've trained her well enough that she can and will.*

She heard her foe coming before he appeared, the slight scrape of metal on stone from the right angle ahead all the alert she needed. She charged forward and rounded the corner with a dagger before her in defense, and the other chambered to stab at whatever she encountered. Another of the metal-and-flesh beings stood before her, this one a woman wearing a torn and tattered dress. The metal had consumed her in a strange diagonal, leaving her head, right arm, and part of her chest flesh, as well as portions of both legs. Her living hand gripped a wand. The other ended in a spike similar to the ones they'd seen already, with the addition of four wicked barbs a few inches back from the tip.

Keshalla stabbed low, attempting to cut into the artery that ran along the flesh leg, but the woman brought her metal arm down to block. The wand snapped forward and discharged a wash of flame. Keshalla calmly summoned a tall barrier of force to deflect the fire past her, then pushed that shield ahead at her opponent. It knocked the witch backward a step. The flames faltered, and Keshalla's defense failed as the woman's wand drank in its power. She stepped ahead and slashed with her left dagger, aiming for the arm, but a force shield intercepted her blow. "You're good. Makes me think our final enemy might be someone to be reckoned with."

She brought the right-hand knife around in a wide strike, and the metal arm again reached up to interpose itself. The move opened the woman's leg, and Keshalla stamped her heel on the floor at the correct angle to extend the hidden blade beneath the toe. She kicked forward and stabbed it deep into her opponent's thigh, then wrenched it to the side. The weapon did more damage coming out than it had going in, and she used the moment of her foe's stunned disbelief at the injury to stab her in the neck with a dagger. The other woman fell, and Keshalla stepped over her without a second thought, flicking her knife to clean it and stomping her foot to retract the blade.

Ruby emerged from her passageway after fighting two more enemies, each almost identical to the first. She'd downed more of her healing potion after each fight and had made a dent in her energy potion to keep her moving. Keshalla stepped out from a different passage a moment afterward. Her teacher asked, "You okay?"

She nodded. "Never better. This is like a vacation. We should come here every year."

Her teacher gestured ahead. "I guess that door is where we're supposed to go."

Ruby turned her head and saw the entrance in question, an ornate barrier of wooden planks and metal bands that looked as if it would fit perfectly in a medieval castle. It was covered with runes and possessed no obvious handle or lock. "Any of that graffiti mean anything to you?"

Her teacher sheathed her weapons. "It's a defensive charm that makes the barrier stronger. It contains lots of threats and warnings as well."

"Awesome. Do we have to decipher it? Some kind of test?"

"Doubtful. Shield yourself." Ruby obeyed instantly,

which was the right choice since the bolts of power Keshalla threw at the door reduced it to splinters. The shards inexplicably flew toward them rather than away, battering their defenses.

When the flying wood had completed its attempt to shred them, Ruby dropped the shield and shook her head. "Subtle. Aren't you the one who always talks about finesse?"

Keshalla shrugged. "Sometimes, you have to overpower an opponent."

"Even if it's a door?"

"*Especially* if it's a door."

Ruby sighed. "I have this vague sense you're trying to use this as some sort of educational experience. If you are, I'm missing it."

Her mentor laughed. "That's different than normal, how?"

Rather than reply, Ruby sheathed her dagger, drew her sword, and headed through the opening into the room beyond.

CHAPTER NINE

The chamber that lay through the doorway was different from any they'd seen so far. It was angular, with enough sides that Ruby didn't know the correct prefix. *Nonagon? Decagon? I think there are twelve.* Each of the flat surfaces, aside from the one housing the entrance, was identically arranged with a waist-high work surface and bookshelves that rose above it to the ceiling twenty feet overhead. Tomes, devices, and abundant unrecognizable objects filled it. The scientist portion of her brain immediately wanted to stay there forever. She breathed, "This is the kind of place you can get some serious research done in."

Keshalla nodded. "It's big enough around that you could do combat training in here, too. Maybe I'll move in when we finish."

Ruby shook her head. "Maybe *I'll* move in after. Speaking of which, doesn't an empty room seem a little anticlimactic?"

Her mentor didn't get the chance to respond. A

scraping voice filled with arrogance asked, "Why have you invaded my workshop?"

Ruby turned a circle, seeking the source, but it seemed to be coming from everywhere. She exchanged glances with the other woman, who shrugged and declined to speak. "Okay, sure, fair question. We're here for an artifact weapon. Perhaps you'd like to hand it over? It would save a lot of time and effort."

Booming laughter echoed from the walls, and without transition, a third figure was suddenly in the room with them. He was completely metal but displayed a softness that hadn't been present in the others they'd faced. His expression moved smoothly as it shifted from humor back to seriousness, making his skin's silver surface look as if it were another hue of flesh. "You mean this?" He gestured, and a sword appeared, a virtual twin to hers, hovering at ceiling height and slowly spinning in the center of the space.

Ruby said, "Aww, there's only one. Guess since I can't wield dual swords yet, it'll have to be mine."

Keshalla shrugged. "Just means I'll have to find the other half of the pair if you fail. Sounds like an interesting quest."

The man snarled, "Silence. You have come to take a sword, but you shall receive only death." A whine entered his tone. "Why will no one listen to my warnings or leave me to my work? Why must you all think you know more than I do when such a thing is obviously impossible?"

Ruby realized that whatever else the figure was, he was insane. *Too much isolation, maybe. I have to remember he's not likely to respond predictably to anything.* Out loud, she replied,

"I don't suppose we could agree that you give us the sword, and we go on our merry way and leave you to your work?"

He extended his right hand. A sudden flash caused both Ruby and Keshalla to step back into defensive poses. When the illumination subsided, he held a large staff, taller than he was, curved and twisted into a strange and uncomfortable spiral. It appeared to be constructed of bone and metal. The former was polished to a blinding white, and the latter shone silver, considerably more brilliant than the dusky gray of his skin. Ruby summoned her force shield around her body and shook her head. "I'm going to skip the lewd joke here and merely say that his weapon looks more well-cared-for than any of the defenses we've seen so far."

He waved his other hand in a lazy circle, and another burst of light filled the room. When it subsided, there were twelve of him present, one for each of the walls. Ruby said, "Dodecagon, that's right."

Keshalla snapped, "Focus," and lurched into motion. All the other figures did as well, casting magic or stepping forward to strike with their staves. Ruby shouted, "Kagji," and her pendant's protective shadow barrier materialized around her. She leapt into a flying kick at the nearest version of their foe and almost lost her balance when she passed through without contact. The figure laughed from behind, and the others echoed the sound. *Guess it was too much to hope the illusions would vanish when struck, right?*

Keshalla whipped her blade through several false versions of the madman until a *clang* sounded as her sword struck the bone-and-metal staff. Another flash of light appeared immediately, and when it faded the figures were rearranged. Ruby yelled, "Not good."

Her teacher replied, "Don't trust vision. Push your senses."

She nodded. It wasn't one of her strongest areas of magic. She had found spare moments to practice, though, and no longer needed to close her eyes to significantly increase the focus of her other senses. The scent of metal came to her from off to her left, a definite clue. Sound was useless since all the figures were babbling, and she wasn't interested in trying to lick any of them, so taste was out. So, she followed her nose and tested the theory with her sense of touch in the form of figure-eight slashes of her sword. Magic slammed off her shields as the man she'd identified blasted power from his staff, and she felt the pendant's protection shred under the impact.

She figured the force shield an inch away from her skin would handle at least one attack, so she continued forward. He shifted the staff into two hands and swiped across at her. She leaned back to let it pass in front of her and took a blast of lightning in the face from the bottom tip. The energy cascaded over her magical defense, seeking a way in. She focused her power into the protective barrier, stabilizing the chips and divots, and moved with the figure as he tried to lose himself among the others in an odd shell game.

Keshalla came in from his backside and stabbed her sword forward in a blow that should have skewered him. He shot up toward the ceiling without warning, and her teacher barely retracted the blade before impaling her with it. The other woman observed, "Apparently being insane gives one interesting battle options. Maybe I've been too hard on you."

Ruby replied, "Shut it." She dipped a hand into her left boot and threw the magic-penetrating knife at the figure. He blocked it with a sweep of the staff and light blazed, obscuring vision. When it faded, there were again twelve cackling crazy people in the room. *This is not going as well as I'd hoped.* Her nose led her toward the real one, and she ignored attacks from all other quarters.

He cackled. "You *are* impressive, almost worthy. When you're defeated and improved, you'll serve as a useful deterrent to whatever fool follows you."

Ruby said, "I don't want to be improved. You're like the magical version of the Borg." Chris Pine was her Kirk, but she had a soft spot in her heart for *The Next Genera-tion.* She blasted a cone of flame from the dagger she'd drawn after throwing the knife and ran forward under its protection, intending to stab him with her sword. He called up a conical shield, judging from the way the fire wrapped around it, but her power had no effect even where it touched him. She skittered to her right and stabbed past the edge of the barrier. Her sword skipped off his metal flesh as if it was the skin of a battleship. Ruby yelled in frustration, "He's unstoppable," and spun out of the path of the staff as it whipped around at her skull again.

Her teacher replied, "No one's unstoppable." She closed and hammered at him with her blades, faster than Ruby had ever seen her move, quicker than she ever hoped to be, even on her best day. Her swords slashed and tested, stab-bing and cutting at legs, arms, and head. Aside from generating sparks and a couple of deep scratches, the attack showed no obvious effect.

The figure laughed again. "Now it is clear who is the master and who the student. It will be instructional for you to see your superior defeated." He shifted his attention to Keshalla. Ruby had no idea what to do other than hope his metal skin was magical because she couldn't conceive of how to get through it otherwise. She sheathed her dagger and her sword simultaneously, then pulled the throwing knife from her boot with her right hand, hiding the point under her outstretched fingers so as not to give him warning if he turned back to her.

She crafted a veil while Keshalla dodged and deflected attacks from their foe. It cost her a moment to ensure the concealment would hold up against all senses, but when it was ready, she slipped ahead quietly. Ruby waited for the opportunity she needed to present itself. When it did, she lunged forward like an Olympic fencer and stabbed the knife into the spot where shoulder and neck joined. The blow had all the brute strength she could put behind it, her hope that between sheer velocity and the weapon's magic it would penetrate his skin. *Please work.*

The blade sank in no more than an inch, but it felt like a victory. She fired lightning at the area, and its touch on his skin was no more effective than her flames had been. Still, the dagger had created a vulnerability, and the electricity traveled through it beyond the protection of his metallic outer layer. He stiffened, rising on his toes, and Keshalla used that second of opportunity to disarm him, slamming both of her swords across in parallel horizontal strikes to knock the staff flying. The mad Mist Elf sank to his knees, clearly in pain. He cackled with a harsh burble. "You will heal me after you fail to master the sword. Then you will be mine." Keshalla stepped over, yanked the knife out of his shoulder, and stabbed it deep into his throat. She blasted her power through it, and he collapsed, his metal features losing their suppleness and turning him into a seemingly lifeless statue.

Ruby collected the thrown blade she'd missed with and slipped it back into her boot. "Well, that sucked. A lot."

Keshalla nodded, holding the other throwing knife in her hand. "He was brilliant. Insane, but brilliant. Such a waste." Her teacher shook her head, then gazed up at the weapon hovering overhead. "By all accounts, you'll have one more battle with the sword. I can't help you with that, but know that I'll be waiting, however long it takes. I'll keep this in case he gets up." She twitched the blade. "Now get to it before something else shows up to try to stop us."

CHAPTER TEN

Ruby extended her telekinesis and pulled the hovering sword down to her. When it touched her palm, everything went white again, as it had when the insane Mist Elf had used his magic. She spun reflexively, swinging the weapon in a circle to defend against any attack that might be on the way. When the brilliance faded, she was no longer in the room, no sword was in her hand, and a figure stood to the side, clapping softly. The Mist Elf woman was dressed in a long flowing gown, had upswept hair piled atop her head, brilliant sapphire eyes, and thankfully not a hint of metal. The stranger said, "Welcome. It is wonderful to have someone finally break the monotony. I did so enjoy your little dance." She delivered the words with bright humor and a smile that stripped them of all offense.

Ruby nodded, surreptitiously scanning the surrounding area for threats while appearing to focus her attention on the woman. "Thank you. I do try my best. What is this place?"

Laughter preceded the explanation. "You could call it

your imagination, I suppose. Or mine. That said, I think a change of setting is in order." She snapped her fingers, and the featureless plane they'd been standing on shifted and slid into a new configuration. What had been cracked earth under her feet was now sand, and ocean waves lapped behind the other woman. Her host lifted the hem of her long dress, slipped off the elegant shoes she wore underneath it and turned toward the water. "Won't you join me?"

Ruby looked down and discovered she no longer wore her armor but a warrior's dress, the skirt slit up both legs for unrestricted movement, and sandals with leather wrappings that extended to her calves. *Okay, sure. This is definitely better than fighting a crazy person who carries a weapon made of people.* She strolled forward until she stood at the woman's side, the comfortably cool water covering their feet. "I'm Ruby, Ruby Achera." When no response was forthcoming, she prompted, "Who are you?"

The other woman's laugh was like a soft bell chiming. "You can call me Shalia."

"How long have you been, uh, here?" Ruby gestured vaguely at their surroundings.

"An eternity, it seems."

Ruby stifled the frown that wanted to rise to her lips at her companion's reticence. "Where were you before this?"

Shalia's face turned thoughtful. "The memories are scattered, like birds buffeted by uncertain breezes. I remember caring for a village. I remember a descent into the mountain, but I can't recall why I did it." She shrugged. "Now, I remember you. Everything in between is foggy and ethereal."

Ruby nodded. The sun hitting her felt nice, and she

thought that maybe a vacation would do her well. *Ha. As if there's time for that. Speaking of which.* "Uh, I don't mean to be rude, but I'm not sure what I'm supposed to do here. Do you know?"

"Of course. You have to win us over."

Okay, who's us? Is that the royal us? "Any clue how I might accomplish that?"

Her host laughed again. "You have already made great progress, Ruby. You've been polite, acceded to my request to share some time in the water, and have given me the honor of your name." She sighed. "Now I must ask the important question, one that will determine whether you have a chance of surviving this experience."

Ruby took an involuntary step backward. "Whoa, whoa, whoa. Survive?"

Shalia turned to her with a soft smile. "Of course. You didn't think the stakes would be any less, did you?"

"Well, I have to admit, given how nice you are, I was kind of hoping for it."

The other woman shook her head sadly. "Unfortunately, I do not control all of this reality, only parts of it. I cannot change the requirements of the test."

Ruby set her feet, turned her face to the sun, and closed her eyes to focus her thoughts. When she felt ready, she opened them and nodded. "All right, then. Fire away."

"You are seeking a weapon of great power. How do you intend to employ it? Will you seek to rule? Will you wreak vengeance upon your enemies? Or will you lock us away in a cabinet against future threat?"

Ruby thought about the question carefully before answering. "It's possible at times that I might engage in all three, I suppose. Sometimes power is necessary, sometimes vengeance aligns with removing a danger that would threaten others, and certainly, every warrior puts up her sword for a time between campaigns. However, my goal, my purpose, is to protect those who can't protect themselves and to defend my chosen home from those who would do its people harm."

"What if your perspective toward your chosen home changes?"

"I'm not the most virtuous person ever, and I certainly suffer from weaknesses, an abundance of them if you believe my family. Still, my purpose is charitable, maybe even noble. I believe if suddenly I could no longer be part of my community, I would find another to serve and defend."

The other woman's face tightened in concern. "Serve? You would acquire an item of power such as this and consider yourself a servant rather than a leader?"

"I would."

She grinned. "Correct answer. You're halfway there. Good luck with the other."

Ruby's reply, "What other?" was lost as the world around her wrenched, the beach scene replaced by a snowy mountaintop. Wind whipped with a keening wail, and she shivered in the provided garments, which were far more suitable for summer than winter. *If this place is partially from my imagination, let's see if I can do something about that.* She focused on what she'd worn beneath the mountain and felt it on her skin. She imagined the outfit was warm and impervious to the elements, and suddenly that was true. Her tightened muscles relaxed.

From behind, a sarcastic snarl observed, "Well done. Of course, even a child could accomplish that." She turned and saw a male Mist Elf dressed in long trousers and a knee-length tunic that recalled what Shalia had worn. "I am Tyrsh. Welcome to my mountain, Ruby Achera."

She snarked, "What's your deal?"

"There's fire in you, excellent." Arrogant laughter colored the words. "I've witnessed your martial prowess in the fight against our creator, as I have observed the few others who reached this place."

"This mountaintop?" It came out a little more sarcastic than she'd intended.

"Don't be an idiot," he snapped. "Only one issue is at hand here. What will you sacrifice to reach your goals?"

She growled, "Is this where I have to say I'm willing to die for my principles?"

Tyrsh countered, "Are you?"

"Not if I can help it. Life is precious and staying alive means living to fight another day. I would not spend that particular coin so casually."

He gave a sharp nod. "Where's the line? Would you die to save one? To preserve ten? A hundred, a thousand, a million? What level of death would be worthy of your oh-so-noble self-sacrifice?"

Ruby put her hands on her hips to avoid throwing obscene gestures at him. His words had undercut her confidence and ticked her off besides. She gathered her remaining calm and exhaled. "It's impossible to know, isn't it? If it were the right person, I would do it without resistance. My sister, for instance. Idryll. Keshalla." She gave a small shrug. "Other than that, such a question will always be situational. Since I'm not precognitive, I can't predict what might happen."

"A deflection," he barked.

She shook her head. "The truth, and nothing but."

His stance changed, relaxing from aggressive to languid. He didn't quite smile, but there was satisfaction in his visage. "You'll do, Ruby Achera. I look forward to seeing what you become. Use us wisely."

She yelled the question at the front of her mind as the feeling of falling overwhelmed her senses. "Are there more than two of you?" No answer was forthcoming, and she snapped back into her body with enough force to fall backward, still holding the sword.

Keshalla was instantly at her side. "Are you okay?"

Ruby sighed as a wave of exhaustion swept over her. "So, you know that thing about artifact weapons being sentient and having a personality?"

She nodded. "I do. Did you get along with it?"

Ruby shook her head, unable to describe the intensity of the experience. "All I can say is that, appropriate to the man who created it, the sword has multiple personalities. And neither of the two I encountered has their full complement of mental marbles."

Her teacher chuckled lightly for a moment, then sat and laughed harder. Eventually, Ruby had to join in. When they had both run out of mirth, Keshalla shook her head. "Well, *minari*, in that case, I can't think of a more appropriate weapon for you."

CHAPTER ELEVEN

Gabriel "The Nightmare" Sloane was not a happy man. In fact, that categorization understated the matter significantly. He was outraged, insulted, and filled with a fury that hadn't left him since the moment the mewling bureaucrat from Magic City informed him they'd denied his petition to build a casino there. *We'll see about that. The letter of the law can be* such *a useful thing.*

Outwardly, he did his best to maintain a normal demeanor, wearing his typical bespoke business suit with a blood-red tie and the most expensive shoes in his closet. A chunky silver bracelet encircled his right wrist and could easily slide down over the knuckles to serve as a weapon. He'd used it before and imagined it was inevitable that he'd someday do so again. A stiletto rested in an inner pocket, more as a remembrance than anything else. A pair of rings, the family seals from two criminal organizations he'd ended, adorned his left hand. He'd killed the head of the first on behalf of the other and the leader of the second as revenge for trying to double-cross him. They all served as a reminder of his roots and a confirmation that whatever happened, he always came out on top.

His wife, Julianna, sat across from him in the back of his limousine. She'd crossed her long legs, and the tight red sheath clinging to her body showed them off to great advantage, right down to the matching stiletto heels. They each held whiskey tumblers filled with the most expensive brand he had on hand. Tonight was important. Tonight was *pivotal*. Whether he was destined to win or lose the war, he would luxuriate in every experience it brought to him, as he had with each challenge life had delivered so far.

His rumination was interrupted by a light knock on the window. He pushed the switch to lower it, and his black-uniformed security guard said, "Perimeter established. Goryo has checked in and says he'll be on time. Trenton is about two minutes away."

Sloane idly swirled the single sphere of ice in his drink. "We don't have tracking on the specialist?"

The sharp-boned and muscular guard with a blond flat-top shook his head. "He switched vehicles. Again."

He chuckled. "Paranoid bastard. I like him. Carry on."

He rolled up the window and asked his wife, "What are your thoughts on all this?"

Her laugh was throaty and sexy, like everything else about her. He found her intelligence every bit as appealing as its container. "I think you should kill Trenton and his pet. Not punishing their failure makes you look too generous."

He shook his head. "Not yet. They're still useful as a distraction. I wholeheartedly agree that they have proven not to be the partners we'd hoped to find in Ely." He was quiet for a moment, thinking through his options. "Perhaps they can at least clear the path for the specialist."

Julianna nodded. "And if he, too, fails?"

Sloane's mouth stretched into a thin smile. "Why, then, we start killing everyone we can find with an interest in Magic City until they give us what we want."

She moved across to sit beside him and planted a light kiss full of promise on his lips. "There's the man I love."

Another discreet knock was a prelude to the door opening. The security agent said, "They're clean, boss." The dwarf was the first one in, followed by his partner. Both looked appropriately nervous, although he sensed an aura of rebellion in the nonhuman. He let the silence stretch, and Trenton babbled, "We're out here in the middle of nowhere. We had to use old-school GPS to find the place. No cell signal at all."

Of course, you idiot, that's why I chose this location. Or, rather, why security chose it for me. "We've had a setback, above and beyond your consistent failures. It's time to get completely serious. Tell me what you're planning to do about the people interfering with our operations."

His wife added, "You better make it perfect. You've failed us too many times." He patted her leg possessively.

While Grentham's expression didn't change, the dwarf's voice sounded like it was on the verge of a tremble as he replied, "We have a good plan."

Sloane interrupted, "You discussed it only in secure locations?"

Trenton nodded. "There is now a protected room at our headquarters. No signals in or out, and an anti-magic emitter, to be sure. Trust me, no one heard about it."

"Well, that's one intelligent move on your part. Continue."

Grentham said, "Those people showed up in person at Spirits, so we think they might have a connection to or preference for that casino. Maybe they were hired as extra protection. We still have the gems we stole from there, so we figured we'd use them as the bait in the trap."

Julianna gave a moan that was on the edge of seductive. "Oh, do say more."

Sloane pushed the distraction of her magnetism away and encouraged, "Indeed, please do."

"Well, we thought we'd bring a fence in to buy the diamonds, set the meeting somewhere that gives us a solid advantage and be sure the details got out to them."

Sloane shook his head. "You faced them before and failed. Do better."

Trenton asked, "What if we let the information slip to all the criminal organizations who were part of the big robbery? They couldn't help but show up, too, and in the chaos, we'd have the perfect chance to take out our targets."

Grentham added, "They won't be able to resist that kind of score. No one will."

Sloane saw the war between the man's greed and his desire for safety in his expression. *Good. Don't forget who you're dealing with, little dwarf. You'll stay alive a bit longer.* He nodded. "Approved. Do it. But keep this in mind: it would be better that you die in the attempt than you fail me again. It's sure to hurt less." The duo bobbed their heads, and he waved them out of the car. When they were alone, he asked his wife, "So, what do you think?"

Julianna shook her head. "I think they won't be around for much longer."

He laughed. "I think the way you think is the most attractive thing about you."

She took his hand and caressed it with a kiss. "Then perhaps you need to be reintroduced to some of the rest."

"I'd like nothing more, but we do have one more person to talk to before we can engage in any indulgences." She gave a playful pout and released him. They chatted about mundane matters until the guard repeated the entry sequence and Goryo slid into the seat across from them. Sloane said, "I hope prison wasn't too much of a burden for you."

The other man chuckled. He was in trousers and a dress shirt and looked more like someone vacationing than he did someone recently released from jail. "It's of no consequence. I have plans in place to deal with such things. Had you not arranged my release, others would have."

"It's a pleasure working with a true professional."

"I feel the same."

Sloane sipped his drink. "Matters have reached a critical point. It's time to go with the endgame option we discussed when I hired you."

The other man nodded, all hints of warmth gone as he shifted into business mode. "Any limits or restrictions?"

"None."

"Very good. You will transfer the agreed-upon sum for this new assignment?"

His wife purred, "Already done."

Goryo gave her a nod that lasted a beat longer than necessary, almost a bow, then met Sloane's eyes again.

"Excellent. I will ensure the ground is prepared for your move."

Back in the house in Ely, Demetrius stared at the feed from his surveillance bots monitoring the guy from the security company and frowned. He muttered to himself, "That's not right. That doesn't make any sense." He triggered several searches to confirm the behavior he saw was indeed unique rather than part of a pattern that occurred over a long enough period that he might have missed it. Unfortunately, the computer confirmed his observation. *Sometimes it sucks, being right all the time.*

He clicked the icon to dial Ruby, knowing she would want the information immediately, but it didn't connect. He sent her a text message asking her to call, then sighed as silence reigned. She'd given him instructions if he needed to get word to her in an emergency, but he'd figured it was a joke at his expense. Only the critical nature of the behavior change in their surveillance target made him willing to go through with it. He left his room, walked upstairs to the attic, and knocked on Ruby's door.

When no one answered, he turned the knob and entered. His girlfriend's cat, Idryll, lay on her back on the bed, seemingly fast asleep. She rolled over as he sat, stretching in that feline communication that clearly indicates anything you might need has to wait until they're good and ready. She sat up primly when the move was complete, her eyes staring straight into his. "Right, okay, this is weird, but Ruby told me if I couldn't reach her with a message, I could tell you." He surreptitiously inspected her, looking for a recorder or a transmitter or something. She didn't wear a collar, so any such device would have to be subcutaneous.

He couldn't imagine that being the case, but he also couldn't figure out what conversing with Ruby's cat would accomplish. "Anyway, the Aces Security people are acting weird. They're not talking as much in general, and they went completely off the grid several times. Either they know they've been bugged or have become paranoid enough to put in some defenses on general principles. I guess they could be vacationing in the middle of the desert on an almost daily basis, but somehow I doubt that."

He smiled at his joke and waited for a response, but the feline continued to stare at him. He stood and patted her head. "Okay, right. Good kitty." They hadn't really bonded, and he figured it was because they competed for Ruby's time. "Do whatever it is you're supposed to do. I'll see you when Ruby gets back."

If he'd looked back as he departed, he would've seen a very un-cat-like smile spreading across the feline's face.

CHAPTER TWELVE

Ruby, Morrigan, and Idryll crossed the street into Margrave's domain. Ruby had a duffel bag thrown over her shoulder filled with stuff to show him, and the shapeshifter was disguised as a human, courtesy of Morrigan's magic. *Three people visiting a friend, nothing to see here.* The animatronics in the yard hadn't changed since their last visit that she could tell, but this time one of them she'd only superficially noticed before caught her eye. A capybara sat on the edge of the porch, occasionally rising on his hind legs to look at them. Ruby was pretty sure it smiled at her, and she shook her head at Margrave's skills. *Someday I'll be that good.*

Her techno-magical mentor opened the door and ushered them inside with a smile. They headed immediately for his basement workshop, where a pot of coffee and mugs awaited their arrival, along with a tray of cookies. Morrigan asked, "You bake?"

He laughed. "Often. It helps me relax." When everyone

was served and seated around the end of his worktable, he gestured at Ruby's bag. "So, did you come bearing gifts?"

Ruby shook her head. "Afraid not, but I did bring you some stuff to look at." She pulled out her new sword first, handing the sheathed weapon to him.

He asked, "May I?" She nodded, and he drew it from its scabbard. It shone brilliantly, and the slightly curved silver blade was etched along its length in symbols and letters. Some were in the Mist Elf language, but others she couldn't decipher. "It's beautiful. Does it have a name?"

"Not yet. I'm working on that."

Morrigan, who was also seeing it for the first time, said, "Man, that's awesome. You totally don't deserve a weapon like that. You should let me take it."

She replied, "Believe me, it comes with challenges. No, you can't have it." He returned it, and she stored it back in the bag. Extracting her costume, she explained, "My teacher on Oriceran, Keshalla, got this for me. It's leather but has clearly been treated with something to increase its flexibility and strength." She passed the smooth tunic and trousers around.

Margrave replied, "Very nice. It would be worth asking if magic was part of the process."

Ruby sighed. "I tried that already. She said, 'Isn't creating such a masterpiece a magic all of its own?'" The others laughed, and she shook her head. "See what I have to put up with? Everyone's a comedian." She stored it back in the bag and handed over her mask. "The tech at the government agency did a great job of integrating new eyepieces and communication devices into this without damaging its power."

He took it eagerly, almost snatching it from her hands, and lifted it to see the lenses in the light. Then he spun in his chair, grabbed a large magnifying glass, and used it to examine the implanted technology. Ruby and her partners traded smiles while he worked, obviously lost in the moment. When he finished, she had already unpacked the next item she wanted to show, and the small drone sat on the table in front of him with its fans rotated out into flight position. He handed back the mask. "This is amazing work. Really good. I'd love to meet whoever did it." He gestured at the item on the desk. "That, on the other hand, is still a work in progress."

Ruby laughed. All the device's insides were exposed since she hadn't yet replaced the pieces she'd removed. She activated the controller, which required two hands to use, and flew the drone around the room. He watched it with a calculating eye and shrugged as it landed. "It's a good beginning, for sure. I already started the printer going based on the schematics you sent and should have the panels in a couple of hours. I had to alter the specs a little because I realized we needed to control for weather. So instead of empty areas between the filaments, I've added a thin membrane. Should keep it waterproof in light rain, at least. If there's a lot of wind, that thing's too small to fly, anyway."

Ruby nodded. "I thought about the wind, but not the rain. Good call."

He accepted the controller from her and piloted the drone in a test circle around the workshop. Frowning at the object in his hands, he observed, "This thing is awkward. And big."

She shrugged. "It's what came with it."

"We can do better. How about you leave this with me, and I'll do the panels and work on the controller?"

"Sure. I have another one to experiment with."

Morrigan interrupted, "Tell him about the electric knuckles things."

Ruby scowled. "I was getting to that. Shut up."

Idryll interjected, "They're like this all the time. Can I move in with you?"

Margrave laughed. "You're always welcome. Unfortunately for you, so are they. I don't think this would be the sanctuary you're hoping for."

The shapeshifter sighed. "Maybe Abbott Thomas will let me live there."

Ruby countered, "Shut up, you. You've never had it so good." She turned back to Margrave. "So, we came across a person who was wearing something that resembled brass knuckles but carried an electrical charge. We thought it might be a nice thing to have, the right amount to render someone unconscious, not enough to kill them or cause permanent damage."

He frowned. "Making the contact point is easily done. Figuring out the best means to power it is less so. I'm happy to work on it. You wouldn't rather have gloves or something?"

Ruby shook her head. "No, I need my sense of touch too much for that."

"Okay. I'll see what I can do. Maybe there's a way to store the charge magically instead of using a battery." Ideas percolated behind his eyes.

"That would be great. We need some nonlethal options."

He replied, "Ancient civilizations used curare darts for that. I'm sure we could whip something similar up. Dosage might be difficult to calculate, though. The literature has the right amount for humans, but there's probably not much study of how it affects magicals. Researching that sounds like fun. I'll take a look."

Morrigan observed, "You have a strange idea of fun, Margrave."

He grinned. "I like what I like. What can I say?"

Ruby said, "There's one more thing I wanted to pick your brain on. We've agreed that we need a base of operations on the surface that's not my house. You must know this area pretty well since you've lived here a long time, so we thought you might have some suggestions."

He frowned and playfully growled, "Because I'm old, you mean."

Ruby put her hand on her chest as if shocked by the accusation. "I would never say such a thing."

"You'd imply it, though."

She spread her hands wide. "Oh, all day long, for sure, imply. But not *say*."

They all shared a laugh at the banter, then he asked, "What are your requirements?"

"Not much. Some space plus utilities for warmth, electricity, and plumbing. Doesn't need to be fancy."

Morrigan added, "It should be secure, and ideally not have too many neighbors who would notice whatever activity might go on."

Margrave snapped his fingers. "I think I know just the spot. Feel like taking a walk?"

It turned out to be a fairly lengthy walk, a couple of miles out into the undeveloped desert beyond Vagrant's Crossing. Finally, they arrived at a dilapidated chain-link fence, wind-blown clean in places, rusty in others. The only thing new about it was the padlock on the gate, for which Margrave produced a key that permitted them entry. "I bought this property, I don't know, twenty years ago or so. Never really had a use for it, but it was too good a deal to pass up. I thought I'd eventually convert it to a workshop, but as technology miniaturized, I needed less space to work. So, I never did anything with it."

Morrigan whispered, loud enough so everyone could hear, "Does he know it's only a big empty field? I think he's crazy."

Ruby couldn't argue with her sister's thinking. "So, *are* you crazy? Is it a mirage? What do you think we should be seeing?"

Idryll replied, "I'm sure he has a reason."

She muttered, "Suck up." The shapeshifter grinned.

Margrave turned to look at them and walked backward. "You know, Mist Elves aren't the only ones who can do disguises. Although mine is a little more technological." He crossed to a patch of scrub, one of several thick growths in the area, and reached inside. Ruby magnified her hearing and sensed the *click* of a button, then quickly killed the magic as the ground nearby rumbled. Dirt and dust danced as the surface vibrated, then retracted to reveal a staircase leading down. "So, there you go, not crazy."

Ruby shook her head. "Not crazier than we already knew you were, anyway."

"Touché. Follow me. Last one in hit the button at the top to close the panel again."

Morrigan asked, "Won't the disturbed dirt be obvious? Even though the door's shut?"

He laughed from ahead, and it echoed strangely in the narrow stairwell. "You'd think so. I put in a few hidden sprayers, and within ten minutes or so, you won't be able to tell there's anything there."

Ruby nodded. "Nice."

Idryll added, "See? Told you he wasn't crazy."

She was distracted from replying as they entered a storage area with metal racks full of boxes. She read the stencil on the side of one. "Meal, Combat, Individual, Spaghetti with Meatballs in Tomato Sauce." She frowned at the man. "Are you now a prepper? Do you think there's a zombie apocalypse coming or something?"

"Ha, ha. Keep moving." He opened a door that wasn't locked and stepped through. The *click* of a switch sounded, and the room's lights tried to come on with a loud snapping noise as she entered. Only about half of the old-style fluorescents from a time long gone by managed the feat. He gestured around at the space. "The very finest in nineteen-sixties decor, am I right?"

It was a living room with couches, chairs, a fireplace, and a large bar along one wall. Even though the stuff was old, it was quality and had endured the years since anyone other than Margrave was inside it exceedingly well. He imitated a realtor's spiel. "This mid-century modern features multiple bedrooms, an exercise area, a couple of offices, plus bathrooms, and a kitchen. It's all outdated, but the rich family that commissioned this place made sure they chose only the best of their era. Everything I've tested still works."

Ruby ventured, "This was a bomb shelter, wasn't it?"

He nodded. "You got it in one. If you looked at your phones, you'd discover that the shell they built around this place blocks signals really well. The only exception is the radio that's attached to an old-school antenna concealed above."

Morrigan observed, "So, no Internet, then. What about television? How were they planning to spend their time underground?"

He laughed. "You can look through the ton of board games in one of the offices, should you get bored. There was a TV, it just no longer works. Even the best nineteen-sixties sets didn't have that long a shelf life."

Ruby said, "This is perfect if you can part with it."

He shrugged. "Here's what I'm thinking. You use the space, do whatever you want with it. When you've finished, I get it back along with any improvements you've made to it. Maybe I'll retire here."

Ruby remembered the twelve-sided room she'd talked about retiring in and shuddered. "Be careful what you wish for. I'm not sure decades underground would be good for you. Does it have other exits?"

He nodded. "A couple, although they're at the ends of long tunnels so they aren't directly associated with this place. One comes out in a deserted building about a half-mile to the west. The other was sealed up at some point by a cave-in, or maybe the demolition of whatever structure was on top of it. You could probably clear it if you cared to."

Ruby looked at her partners. "I think this will do nicely. Agree?"

Morrigan shrugged. "At least you'll know where your bags are."

She made an obscene gesture at her sister and turned to Idryll. "And you?"

She beamed. "When you're annoying, I can send you here where you won't be able to bother me. It's ideal."

Ruby shook her head. "With friends like this, who needs enemies?" She clapped her hands together as excitement blossomed inside her. "You got yourself a deal, Margrave. Now, let's talk about what we need to do to get this place ready for action."

CHAPTER THIRTEEN

Ruby let herself flop back on the bed and whined, "How can you keep working when your oh-so-beautiful-and-talented girlfriend is right here?"

Demetrius, positioned in front of his multiple monitors with his hands flying over the keyboards, laughed without turning to look at her. "I told you I had to work today. Was that not clear?"

"You're a freelancer. You can work whenever you want."

He snorted. "Ah, the myth of the independent contractor. What being my own boss means is that, when someone goes to the effort to arrange actual plans ahead of time," he paused, ensuring she knew which *someone* he was referring to, "I can block off my calendar to make sure I'm free. At the moment I have a deadline, and it's soon."

"But I'm *right here*. Don't you understand?" Since returning from Oriceran with her new weapon, Ruby's spirits had been unusually high. She didn't expect anything of Demetrius but enjoyed teasing him now and again. *Gotta keep him on his toes, right?* "Do you know how many men would pass on an opportunity like this? Not very many, let me tell you."

"So, you're saying you've had a lot of boyfriends then?"

She frowned. "I don't see how that's relevant."

He laughed. "I've spoken with your sister several times. She's made it clear that you're not particularly experienced with long-term romantic relationships. Or, really, have had any practice at all."

"She should shut it. *You* should shut it. *Everyone* should shut it."

He observed, "You're needier than your cat. By the way, how did she get the message to you?"

Ruby grinned. "Trade secret. Seriously, man, I'm bored. Quit working."

A tone sounded from his computers, and whatever he was about to reply went out the window. "Looks like you won't be bored for long. That was the email account you set up for the sheriff. She wants to meet as soon as possible."

Ruby sighed. "Fine. Be that way." She got up from the bed with a groan and gave him an embrace from behind that was part-hug and part-choke based on where her arms wound up. She kissed the top of his head. "You owe me a date. Figure out what, where, and when. I'm not some feckless floozy you can toy with at random." She imitated a movie starlet about to burst into tears. "I'm, I'm… Vulnerable." He laughed. She responded in kind and headed out to work. "Keep it real, Tree. I'm serious about the date."

While Ruby trusted Sheriff Valentina Alejo as much as she did anyone outside her inner circle, there was always the possibility the PDA might pressure her or that they could have an eye on her without her knowledge. Thus, agreeing to meet at a specific time and place was a bad idea. Instead, she portaled to a building near the sheriff's department in her disguise and used the high-powered microphone Margrave had provided for her incursion into the security company that seemed so long ago to listen to the goings-on in Alejo's office.

After thirty minutes of boring conversations, the woman told the other person in the room with her that it was time to get a snack, and a full minute of silence followed the sound of the door closing. Ruby packed away the device. *If this is a trap, it's an impressive one since she doesn't know I'm coming. I think this is about as safe as I can manage.* She summoned a veil and made her way to the building. Alejo's office had a window, and it required minimal telekinetic effort to undo the latch. She extended the veil that concealed her to include the window, so if it generated any noise it wouldn't be noticed and lifted it. After climbing into the room, she closed the opening behind her.

Alejo's area was neat and precise, like the woman herself. Her desk was wood topped with plastic or glass, and perfectly aligned piles of paper rested at each of the far corners. The space in front of the chair held a laptop displaying a lock screen. All four walls were adorned with pictures of people and interspersed with accolades Alejo had earned. A martial arts trophy sat on a table in the corner, and Ruby approached to read it. *First place, North-*

west Regional Jujitsu Tournament. Not bad. Ruby arranged herself on the couch, which was old leather and surprisingly comfortable despite—or because of—its demonstrably heavy use. She firmed up her veil and enhanced her senses in case she was in the jaws of an elaborate trap.

Ten minutes later, Alejo returned with a mug of coffee and moved to her desk, settling in with a sigh. Ruby extended the sound dampening to include the whole room, added a sight shield so no one would see anything unusual through the window, then released the personal veil around her. Fortunately, she'd waited until Alejo's hand was away from the coffee cup because the other woman started and jerked at her appearance. Ruby said calmly, "Sorry. Didn't mean to alarm you. I can't be sure the PDA isn't watching you, so I needed to visit unannounced."

Alejo took her time responding, bracing herself with a sip from the mug. "Well, I did ask you to come, so I guess I can't complain. First, I wanted to thank you for your efforts at the warehouse. A lot of people could've gotten hurt without your help, and that's all the PDA would've needed to expand their influence in Ely. They're champing at the bit to step up, and I don't think it's good for any of us if they do."

Ruby frowned. "Are they actively investigating the warehouse incident?"

Alejo snorted. "They're trying their best to. Fortunately, they don't have jurisdiction, and we've been able to keep them away from the people we arrested." She shook her head. "Not that any of them are talking in any case. They must either be pretty scared of their boss or well-paid."

"How about your informant?"

She leaned back in her chair and crossed her arms. "He says he did what we wanted, and now we should leave him alone."

Ruby lifted an eyebrow. "Will you?"

The other woman laughed. "Of course not. Once you're on the hook, you stay on the hook. Anyway, that's not why I asked to meet."

She stood, walked around the desk, and perched on the edge facing Ruby. "There's a lot of chatter in the air about a big opportunity coming up. Apparently, a bunch of the stolen gems from the casinos, particularly Spirits casino, have been gathered together. Whoever has them plans to hand them over to a big-time fence who's visiting town for the deal."

Ruby frowned. She'd been checking on the precious stones at least once a day with her tracking magic, but nothing useful had come of it. They'd remained scattered, unchanging. *This development must've happened very recently. She couldn't remember the last time she'd done it, but surely it was after she got back from Oriceran. Or maybe not. That would've been stupid. Oh well, irrelevant.* "Where? When?"

"The word is tonight, after dark, nothing more detailed than that. The where, though, no idea. Once that information gets out, and it's sure to since everyone's watching everyone else, we can probably assume mayhem will result as everybody goes after the diamonds. That's going to be seriously ugly."

Ruby sighed. "You're right, of course. Do we care if a bunch of criminals winds up fighting among themselves?" *She* cared but wasn't sure that Alejo needed to.

The sheriff nodded. "It's officially on the radar, so a response is required. Given how big it is, we'll have to do so in force."

"Which means you have to work with the leaky Ely PD, which means anyone who doesn't already know will soon, including the PDA. You realize it's probably a trap set for me, right?"

The other woman shrugged. "Yeah, that occurred to me. So I'm not sure whether I'm warning you off or telling you what we'll be doing so you can supplement our efforts. I can guarantee you that my people and I will be there in force. I'm positive you're correct that the PDA will as well. The only chance we have of avoiding a bloodbath might be an unexpected move that takes out the gems or the key people who will cause the most trouble."

Ruby sighed. "Okay. I hear you, and I'll be there. Not sure what I can do, but at least we'll be able to figure it out together. I'll contact you when I'm in range. You contact me through the email address if anything changes. Now, if you'd be so kind as to leave the room, I'd rather no one witnessed my Batman-esque vanishing skills."

Alejo laughed. "Seriously, though, be careful."

Ruby nodded. "Always."

***

Ruby returned to her parents' house in the kemana. The underground city often seemed to give her more precision with her magic. Whether that was true or a subjective perception, she wasn't sure. Either way, she'd take any help she could get. She dropped into lotus position on the bed, and Idryll sat back-to-back with her in her tiger-woman form. Contact with her partner calmed her, and she needed every available advantage for what she was about to do.

Before, she'd been vaguely able to sense the locations of the gems and thus know that they weren't together. Now she wanted to try to pinpoint their location. If she could figure out where they were and retrieve them during the day, it would take the night's activities right off the table and keep everyone safe. She closed her eyes and fell inward, visualizing a map of the area as seen from above. *Heh. Magical Google Maps.* She released her magic, envisioning it flowing up through the ground and riding on air currents, looking for the stones it connected to.

It took a while, but eventually, she got a sense of where the diamonds were and groaned at the discovery. They were together, as Alejo had said. Unfortunately, they were also moving. While her magic would've been adequate to nail down their position if they were stationary, she couldn't track them in motion without a great deal of effort—energy and time she wouldn't be able to expend while pursuing them. She considered whether she could guide Morrigan and Idryll into position, but after several minutes of trying to improve her connection to the gems, she released the magic in disgust.

Idryll asked, "Not quite what you'd hoped for?"

Ruby let her head fall gently back against the shapeshifter's. "Nope. I hoped to find a safer way to do this, but I don't think there is one."

"You won't be foolish enough to leave me behind this time, right?"

Ruby laughed. "Oh, hell no. I wouldn't dare go into this battle without you by my side."

"Good. You're getting smarter."

"This is big enough that I'll have to invite Morrigan along too. I think a trip to visit Diana and her people is in order. Better get this ball rolling."

CHAPTER FOURTEEN

Goryo wasn't in the habit of conducting his business in the daytime hours, but coordinating the various pieces of his operation required such sacrifices from time to time. He was dressed in a casual suit, no tie, and wore an ID badge that proclaimed him a reporter for a gaming website. He had several items with him that pretended to be something they were not: a phone, an audio recorder, and a small Bluetooth keyboard. Each would be important to the success of the endeavor ahead. Also hidden in his watch was a tiny USB chip that was exactly what it appeared to be. Those objects would be useful once he passed beyond the outer cordon of protection, but he needed to bluff his way through to get there.

Fortunately, he was skilled at every part of his vocation, including acting and spycraft. He slid the apparently innocuous items onto the conveyor belt and walked through the metal detector, nothing on him sufficient to set it off. From an average person's perspective, the security of the building would seem tight. A black-uniformed guard patrolled the lobby, his gun belt holding a pistol and a taser, and another like him waited beyond the checkpoint.

In truth, it was lighter than it should've been, but that was because the people who clandestinely operated in the space relied on concealment. *Foolish, in an age of infomancy.* His final concealed item was disguised as a hearing aid in his right ear that would connect him to Scimitar, his frequent associate in computer-related endeavors.

He walked out of the UNLV Research and Technology Park building lobby and found the esports arena beyond it, as expected. It had two parts, a broadcast studio behind a pane of glass complete with anchor desk and control room, and the actual space where the gamers competed. It was all in the name of research on behalf of a casino wanting to stake a claim in that area, but it was also an authentic functioning venue. No casino would miss the chance to monetize their research. He approached an empty station under the guise of examining it and was intercepted by a redheaded female PR person in a sapphire business suit, white blouse, and heels.

Goryo plastered on a broad smile and spoke in a fake California accent. "Hi, I'm Steve Adretti, as you can see from my badge." He laughed as he tapped it, and the PR person nodded as she peered down at the tablet in her hands.

"You're on the list. Always happy to welcome reporters from *Max Queue Gaming.* Any questions I can answer for you today?"

He gestured at the machine. "What kind of specs are you running?"

She offered a professional smile that suggested people asked that question far too often. "Standard stuff, off-the-shelf. How about I give you a press kit with that information in it so there are no worries about accuracy? As you can see, our gamers are competing in a tournament. The game is one we created ourselves, set among the casino's properties. It's basically a big scavenger hunt, with tricks and traps that the competitors can use against each other."

Goryo nodded. "Sounds interesting and challenging. Are they taking to it well?"

She gestured at the giant display at the far end of the room. "See for yourself." The screen showed feeds from all the computers. The competitors did seem to be giving their all, each trying to gather all the relevant clues or prizes or whatever the game's point was. He didn't care, and part of him wanted to start killing people rather than deal with this woman any longer. Instead, he inappropriately sat on the edge of the counter next to the empty computer and forced a smile. "How about I wait here and think of some more questions while you grab me that press kit?"

She nodded and headed for a small podium that stood behind the door. He retrieved the USB chip from the underside of his watch and slipped it into the back of the machine, pretending to examine the connectors. After ten seconds, a soft *ping* sounded in his ear. He pulled out the chip, straightened with a smile, and took the packet the woman offered. "Is it okay if I wander back and take a look at the broadcast studio, Miss Carson?"

She generated a smile as plastic as his. "I'll take you there myself." At that instant, her cell phone rang, and she raised a hand as she answered it. With a frown, she said, "I received an important message from the home office. I'm afraid I'll have to go. There's another representative inside the control room. Tell them I sent you." He had already noticed the easy back-and-forth traffic flow between the two areas.

Goryo offered his thanks and headed for the passage beyond. He muttered, "Nice job with the distraction."

Scimitar's computer modulated voice replied, "No problem. I had the list of people working the event, so as soon as you said her name, it was simple. I'm fully into the upper-level system. Publicizing that they use their whole facility as a server farm to help with their esports events wasn't such a smart move security-wise, although it probably got them a couple more dollars from technology investment companies. Morons."

Once through the passage, he turned left instead of right, heading away from the esports area toward a service corridor that ran through the back. He wondered, as he often did, who Scimitar really was. She had told him she was female early on, but otherwise, he hadn't been able to find out anything about her. He admired that fact and trusted her as much as he trusted anyone. She was the one who would have gotten him out of prison if the others hadn't.

The infomancer reported, "I have cameras. Two guards ahead in front of the elevator. They're carrying pistols and tasers, plus radios, of course."

"You can jam them?"

The woman gave a static-filled laugh. "Honey, I was born able to jam radios. Child's play. Literally."

He shook his head, imagining what that sort of childhood would be like, then focused on the moment as he rounded the corner and saw the guards. He raised his voice, friendly and confident. "Oh. Hey guys. I seem to have missed a turn somewhere, or the PR person sent me in the wrong direction. Can you tell me how to get to the casino floor simulation?"

One replied, and both kept hands near their weapons. He pretended not to hear, turning his head so they could see the hearing aid. He cupped his ear to make sure the message got through. Each step of feigned confusion brought him closer to the guards, but their level of alarm didn't rise, clearly willing to accept that he was what he seemed. *Probably they deal with idiots like this all the time.* When one of them lifted a hand, palm out, it was time to move.

Goryo raced forward at that one, who had moved slightly nearer than his colleague, and channeled his momentum into a flying sidekick that took him in his bulletproof vest. It knocked the man stumbling backward, which was the goal of the move. He landed smoothly and delivered an elbow to the other's temple, who had foolishly gone for his taser rather than his gun. The blow stunned him enough that Goryo was able to grab the hand holding the taser, aim it at the first guard, and push down on the captive finger until the weapon discharged. He finished the standing one with another elbow, then kicked the one now on the floor thanks to the stun gun, rendering him unconscious.

He attached the false audio recorder to the panel outside the elevator doors, and they parted a moment later.

It was the work of a minute to drag the bodies inside and position them out of easy view. "You can keep them locked up in here? Or do I need to kill them?"

"I have them. No worries. The car has a suppression system built-in, so if they get ornery, I'll gas them."

He nodded. "Okay. Going down."

CHAPTER FIFTEEN

Now that he'd entered a space he definitely shouldn't be in, Goryo needed to move with deliberate speed. He stripped one of the men of his bulletproof vest and gun belt, slipping them on as the elevator dropped. The display had ceased giving floor numbers, but he trusted Scimitar would deliver him to where he needed to be. According to the blueprints acquired at great expense from a worker at the construction company who had built the facility's underground portion, three separate laboratory spaces awaited him. His source in the Paranormal Defense Agency, who was equally expensive, had let slip that weapons research happened at the facility, which was the inspiration for his incursion. Given the magical opposition he'd faced so far in Ely, he wanted to be as well-outfitted as possible, and the facility's proximity made the decision to infiltrate it easy. *Once I've finished here, there will be only one more item on my acquisition list. Then I'll be ready to launch the operation phase.*

The door opened, and he strode forward as if he

belonged. The corridor was brightly lit with government-issue fluorescents overhead and had utilitarian linoleum on the floor. He muttered, "Guess they didn't go for the same expensive flash down here as upstairs."

Scimitar replied, "I'll have to take your word for it. I couldn't get past the elevator controls upstairs."

He put on a bored expression, as if he was another guard on patrol, and located all three labs. One was indeed labeled "Weapons," a second, "Info," and the last, "Biology." He whispered, "It looks as if your sources were correct, too." The possibility of infomancy research happening in the facility had made joining too tempting for her to refuse. *Professionals always seek to improve by whatever means they can.* He pulled out the item that looked like a phone but wasn't and pressed it against the touchscreen outside the door that Scimitar was most interested in. The portal popped open, and he pocketed the device.

Inside, computers arranged in clusters of five surrounded central poles providing power and connection. There were three such groupings, but only one was full at the moment. Five beings sat in chairs with large VR masks over their eyes. *Convenient. Maybe they'll even get to live through this if they stay distracted long enough.* A control panel in one corner separated a pair of researchers from the main part of the room. He walked around behind them and saw displays of what each of the infomancers viewed in their headsets. He couldn't make heads or tails of it, but infomancy had never been an area of study for him. *I prefer to leave that to the professionals.* A researcher twisted to face him with a frown. "Something we can do for you? Shouldn't you be on patrol or something?"

He gave a thin smile. "Arrogant. Elitist. Rude." He whipped his elbow around for another temple smash, and the man went down. Before his colleague could react, Goryo had him on both knees in a wrist lock. "Cause me trouble, and I'll break your arm, then kill you both. Understand?"

The man stammered, "Yes, yes, understood. "

"Good." With his free hand, he withdrew the Bluetooth keyboard, the largest disguised object he had brought, and set it on the console.

After thirty seconds that felt ten times that long, Scimitar announced, "I have access. Three people in the biology lab and five in the weapons area."

"And the emergency exit?"

"As we were told. A tunnel with a golf cart ready and waiting to carry you to the egress."

I love it when things work as they're supposed to. "Okay. Any alarm response yet?"

"None. Be sure to take the keyboard with you. I've downloaded a ton of goodies to it."

He laughed softly. "Of course." It was decision time. The smartest thing to do would probably be to go into the weapons area, kill everyone inside, and make off with what he'd come to get. However, discovering the biological research facility intrigued him. *Knowledge of one's enemies can be as valuable as a weapon, if not more so.* He decided to risk checking it out, suspecting that any such work would be investigations of or experiments on magicals.

A kick rendered the man unconscious, and he departed the room, leaving the infomancers in their ridiculous helmets none the wiser. He walked briskly into the biology lab. It took hardly any time at all to defeat the two soft scientists within. He was ready to put down the third disguised device, but Scimitar directed, "Use the keyboard instead." He complied, and a moment later, she reported, "Downloading. The programs I stored in it work like a dream. I'll refund half the cost of this run, as agreed, when you turn it over."

He thought about bargaining, for fun, but didn't. "Excellent. Will we finally meet in person?"

She laughed. "I like you, buddy, but no. I haven't lived this long by being overly trusting." A few seconds passed before she confirmed, "Download complete. Leave the other device there so I can maintain access." Normally, her incursions would have rung alarm bells, but the first thing she'd done to their system was to inject a virus that made it appear she was one of the infomancers working to defend the place. Or at least that's what she'd explained. He didn't care, as long as it worked.

He did as instructed, and she laughed. "Oh, they really were concerned about security. They put the suppression systems in all the labs. Standby." A couple of minutes went by before she said, "Everyone in the weapons area is down. The gas has dissipated enough for you to go in."

He smiled up at the room's camera. "I like you more and more with every passing moment."

She laughed. "Flatterer. Move."

He obeyed. She opened the door through the network and setting the keyboard on the control panel allowed her to pop the locks on all the cabinets in the room. He moved from one to the next, examining the options. There was too much to carry it all away, and he hadn't been able to smuggle in a bag. He'd be limited to what he could reasonably fit into one of the storage crates already present in the room. It didn't matter. He sought quality, not quantity. He took boxes of anti-magic bullets to start. *Always useful.* The next cabinet revealed grenades, and when he read off the model number, Scimitar said, "Whoa. They're filled with anti-magic shrapnel wrapped around standard explosive. That's mean."

He chuckled as he gathered up the four that were present. "Only a matter of time before someone figured that out, I guess." The next cabinet was twice as wide as the others and held guns resting upright on shallow shelves. The top one was a machine gun, the middle an assault rifle, but the one on the bottom caught his eye. He pulled out the shotgun and the box of shells for it. "Looks like a variation on a theme. I bet the pellets are the same ones as in the grenades."

He discovered nothing interesting in the next couple of cabinets, only prototypes that didn't appear functional. The final cabinet contained only a single heavy backpack. He read off the code number. Scimitar sounded slightly alarmed as she reported, "It's a portable anti-magic emitter. Pretty heavy, but I've never seen one that miniaturized that's also that powerful."

He shrugged it on and found that while it was indeed heavier than he would've preferred, it wasn't a significant burden. "Okay, I have all I can carry. Get me out of here."

CHAPTER SIXTEEN

Ruby was impressed by Diana Sheen's office. *Okay, to be fair, everything about her has impressed me so far, so why should this be any different?* It was a combination of practical and stylish that fit perfectly with what she understood of the other woman. A battered wooden government-issue desk sat in the corner, presenting a workmanlike appearance with a high-tech-looking chair behind it. A couple of couches and end tables filled the majority of the space. The wall covered with a massive electronic display was the room's dominant feature. She could easily picture strategy sessions going on around it, although she'd heard some mention of a particular place in the facility where that happened. *Someday, I'd like a real tour, both front of house and back of house, to put it in casino terms.*

Sheen herself sat on the couch arranged at a right angle to her own. She was in beat-up jeans, scuffed jump boots, and a concert T-shirt with a picture of Robert Smith's lipstick-smeared face on it. The agent observed, "You realize this totally sounds like a trap."

Ruby snorted. "Yeah, I said the same thing to Sheriff Alejo. She's still planning to be there tonight."

The other woman shook her head. "Appropriate, doing her job as she should, but also stupid. Unfortunately, sometimes the job is like that."

"Which is why we'll be there too. If we don't show, the police will get creamed."

Sheen shrugged. "Is that your problem? No offense, but you're not with any agency that would be required to be a part of this."

Ruby gave a sharp nod. "I've made it my problem."

The response earned a smile. "That's an answer I both understand and respect. What do you need from us?"

She sighed. As much as she hated to admit it, the situation could quickly go out of control despite her best efforts. "Anything you can provide. This one worries me. I've never had to deal with so many moving parts all banging around at the same time."

"So you expect the sheriff's people, the Ely PD, you and your team, and whoever's selling the gems to show up?"

Ruby nodded. "Probably the PDA too. And, if the word gets out, which it already has, we're going to see individual criminal groups from all over the place converge for a shot at the diamonds."

Sheen leaned forward attentively. "What's your specific plan?"

She matched the motion, eager to hear what the other woman thought of her plan. "I thought we would shoot in, grab the gems, and get the hell out. With the motivation behind the whole event gone, there won't be any reason for the bad guys to continue."

The agent shook her head with a frown. "That would be a good solution if you're able to hit them beforehand. There's still time. Can you?"

Ruby sighed. "They're in motion, and I can't track them properly. It was a paranoid move on their part that's paying off big time in screwing things up for us."

"Well, then, everyone will think the gems are still there and keep fighting to get them, or by that point, they'll be too bloodthirsty to stop. Once it kicks off, simply removing the initial catalyst isn't going to fix it." She lapsed into silence for almost a full minute, her face showing deep thought. Despite her strong desire to interrupt, Ruby restrained herself. Finally, the agent said, "I'll run it by my team, but it seems to me the optimal solution is for us to try to take out the leaders of each group and hope their followers fall back."

She kept her voice level. "Us?"

The other woman nodded. "Yeah. I think we'll join you for this one. Best case, we get more insight into the black-market artifact trade from the people we round up, and we help out a friend. Worst case, we assist in keeping you alive and out of the PDA's hands."

Ruby scowled. "I don't suppose you can do anything about them? They're beyond annoying."

Sheen laughed. "No. Believe me, if I had that much power, they'd already be disbanded. There are some good people in that organization, but they aren't the ones currently calling the shots."

She replied, "I've only met the jerks."

"They have a lot of them, for sure. As a professional

courtesy, one government agency to another, we do see killing them as off-limits."

"Yeah, us too. We try to remain nonlethal wherever we can, but draw a hard line where law enforcement and the like are concerned."

Sheen nodded. "Good. That's how it has to be. So, we have several things to accomplish. Between now and this evening, we have to identify the leaders of each criminal organization. I'll have Deacon hack the Ely PD again and see what they have, but it would probably be more respectful to request that same information from the sheriff's office instead of taking it. Can you make that happen?"

"Pretty sure. Keep hacking them as a backup, and I'll reach out to Alejo as soon as I'm back."

"Okay, so I think we'll coordinate our actions, but as discrete units rather than a single team. You and your people haven't had an opportunity to train with me and mine, and we don't know enough about one another to be interdependent in the chaotic scene this will doubtless be. We'll need to make sure that everyone who needs to be connected by comm, is. Before you leave, talk to Kayleigh. She can unlock the full capability of the communicators we gave you, which includes setting up separate channels on a far more expansive basis than their current mode allows."

Ruby offered a mock frown. "You mean you gave us a present but didn't let us have all of it?"

Sheen laughed. "Yeah, more or less. Listen, my people have all been burned often enough by those we trusted that now we play it as cool as we can, whenever we can."

"I'm joking. You all have been amazing, and I'm totally happy with whatever you share with us."

"We should consider bringing you in for some real training sessions, though. It would be good if at least a couple of us were able to fit in seamlessly with what you're doing. Speaking of which, since you're all in disguise, we'll mask up, too. Don't want to give away who you're working with, just in case." She laughed. "My team has done a lot of weird things, but we've never worked with masked vigilantes before."

Ruby chuckled. "I'd prefer crusader to vigilante, please, even if the other is technically accurate."

Sheen nodded. "Fair enough. I would in your place, too. I'd be lying if I said my team and I always operated within the bounds of rules and regulations. Sometimes you have to improvise."

That drew a surprised laugh from Ruby. "You know, that's the best description ever. I feel like I've been improvising since the moment I got back to Magic City."

"Another thought, we'll want to make sure we're able to track one another. Tell Kayleigh you need a transponder chip, too. You can discuss with her the most effective way to integrate it into your costume."

Ruby shook her head with a grin. "That sounds like Halloween. We prefer battle dress."

Laughter rang out, and she appreciated how quickly the other woman moved between seriousness and mirth. *Although, with Rath around, she probably gets a lot of joy in her life.* Sheen replied, "Well, fair enough. We make some interesting semantic choices here from time to time as well. It would certainly be unfair to stop you from doing the same thing." She turned sober again. "Anything else you can think of equipment-wise that you might need from us?"

"Maybe once we've trained together, I'll have a better answer for that. Right now, adding something new to the mix would probably cause more confusion than benefit."

Sheen nodded and rose, signaling the end of the meeting. "We have work to do, so let's get to it. Visit Kayleigh and talk to Alejo. Once your transponder's on, we'll know where you are, but go ahead and share the location as soon as you have it. We'll do our best to be in place before anything kicks off."

"Us too. Thank you again for all of this."

The agent grinned. "One truth you'll learn about my team is that we live for this sort of thing. Mixing it up, making a difference. It's our purpose, both officially and personally."

"Sounds like I'd fit in pretty well with y'all." She rose and extended a hand to meet the one the other woman had offered.

"Who knows? Stranger things have happened. When your work's finished in Ely, we can talk." Sheen took her hand in a strong grip and shook it. "For now, though, get moving. Daylight's burning."

CHAPTER SEVENTEEN

Ruby threw her bag onto one of the last-century couches in the bunker's main room and looked around in disbelief. "This place is amazing. It's going to take weeks of serious effort to get it completely functional, though."

Morrigan did the same with her duffel and nodded. "Well, we're all chock-full of free time, right?"

Idryll, who had perched on the arm of one of the couches, replied, "I am."

Ruby pointed at her. "Perfect. You're elected. You can live here until it's clean." The shapeshifter bared her fangs, and she laughed. "Hey, you volunteered."

Idryll started to say something, but Ruby lifted a hand to stop her as the tiny device in her ear activated with a soft *ping*. In addition to the transponders, Kayleigh had given her three earbuds so they could have access to communication when not wearing their masks. The units were the next best thing to invisible, and if anyone noticed them, the tech had suggested they use the excuse of excessive ear wax treatment. Ruby was pretty sure she'd been joking, but sometimes it was hard to tell.

Demetrius said, "Okay, people. I got a hit from the bugs. The other dude, not the one we planted them on, used the phrase 'putting our enemies on the scrapheap.' Our guy laughed as if it was funny, and that started me thinking. The only thing that qualifies as a scrapheap around here is the Casino Graveyard."

Ruby replied, "That seems worth following up on. Let me get in touch with Alejo, and I'll tell you what she says." She gave the verbal commands to switch channels and initiate the call to the sheriff. Her unit automatically added the voice modifications that the mask created when she wore it. The comms used heavy encryption plus jumped through a series of hoops to disguise location. Kayleigh had assured them they were untraceable. They'd left their cell phones at home so they couldn't be tracked to the bunker.

The sheriff said, "Alejo. Who is this?"

Ruby replied, "Do you recognize my voice?"

She heard the frown. "Yeah. What have you got for me?"

"Rumor is it might be the Casino Graveyard."

"Wait a second, let me check something." The sound of a keyboard came over the line for a moment, then she continued, "That makes sense, based on what we've collected of people's movements. Plus, it fits the criteria we talked about. For a trap, I mean."

Ruby laughed darkly. "Yeah, I know. Picture-perfect, for that. Keep me updated if anything changes. I'm watching the email."

"You do the same." The other woman clicked off.

She informed Demetrius and her partners that the sheriff agreed with his guess. He said, "I'm sending a drone now. I'll have pictures for you in five minutes or so."

Ruby grabbed her duffel. "Time to unpack. Masks first, in case he has something he wants us to see." As well-shielded as the place was, it didn't block the equipment they'd gotten from the agents. She started taking the items out of her bag and laying them carefully on the couch. When she set the sword down, Idryll hopped off her perch and took the sheathed weapon, examining it with interest. "So, it talks to you?"

"Not really. Only the once. Although sometimes I think I can hear something, right at the edge of my senses, that might be them. It. Whatever." She waved a hand. "Now's not the moment to discuss it." By the time they had all of their gear arranged, Demetrius was back on the line. She slipped on her mask and motioned for the others to do the same, and he fed them video from the drone.

He apologized, "It's really high up, so you're not going to have too much detail, but I didn't want to give anyone a warning that we were looking at them."

"Good call." Castoffs generated by the construction and reconstruction of Magic City covered a large flat expanse of desert. It was a labyrinth of shipping crates, piles of discarded building materials, dated cars and trucks that didn't survive the process and had nowhere else to go, and tons of heavy equipment. The tallest object was a crane that rose into the sky, held steady by guy wires at four anchor points. From it hung a large claw that was used in the operation's working days to move debris into the giant crusher located near the center. The graveyard hadn't been active for twenty years or so, although new deposits had accumulated as casinos were modified or demolished and rebuilt anew.

Morrigan observed, "That's bad news. There are tons of places to hide out in there if it's a trap."

Ruby nodded. "Completely true. It's quiet now, though, or at least looks that way. We need to get in, go to ground and figure out what advantages we have." She continued, "Thanks, Tree," then killed the channel and removed the mask.

The others did the same, and Morrigan laughed. "Your nickname for him is Tree? There are so *many* things I could say about that."

Ruby shook her head. "Not the time. Save it for after." It was a mark of her sister's concern for the danger they faced that she obeyed. "Let's gear up. Then we'll figure out how best to get there."

Morrigan replied, "No worries on that front. I've been there when Spirits dropped off some renovation junk. I can portal us outside the office trailer."

Ruby nodded. "Excellent." She donned her base layer of supple Oriceran leather. Boots went on next, carefully laced to ensure they wouldn't slip. She stuck her knives inside them, inspecting each to verify they were undamaged from the battle against the mad Mist Elf scientist. Her belt followed. It was growing heavy with all the stuff attached to it. *I really do need to find some time for strength training. Maybe I'll see if my work at Spirits can be carrying around heavy things.* She wasn't looking forward to investing that time, but Daphne's joy at being told of the arrangement—Ruby's ongoing contribution carefully not mentioned—made the investment more than worthwhile.

She strapped the holster down to her right thigh and thought she'd probably be better off if she could learn to shoot with her offhand. *Sure, sure. Maybe I can make that part of my Spirits gig as well.* She inwardly snorted as she scrutinized the pistol magazine, then inserted it into the empty weapon and racked the slide to chamber a round. She pulled the magazine back out and slipped one more anti-magic bullet into it, then reseated it and stored the gun in its holster, securing the tie-down. The dagger was already in its sheath at her left hip, but she drew it and checked it for damage as well. Next up was a touch on each of the grenades, two concealment and two lightning, all she could fit because of the other stuff she was carrying. *Add a redesign of my equipment to the list. Honestly.*

Morrigan interrupted her reverie. "Why are you making that face?"

She turned to see that her sister was almost ready. "Just thinking how nice it would be to have a clone. Someone I could send to do the work I need to do or even use as a partner. It'd be a huge improvement from working with you."

Morrigan rolled her eyes. "Sick burn. Maybe your clone should take lessons on insulting others because you *suck* at it."

Ruby countered, "Well," then paused, finding no more words. "I have nothing to say to that. Shut up."

Her partners laughed as Ruby checked to make sure her flasks were in her belt pouch. Her fingers encountered the battery that was the terminal point for the thin cable that ran under the back of her tunic and out through her left sleeve. A small connector dangled at the end. She slipped on the metal knuckles Margrave had deposited for them in the bunker. Her hand flexed easily, and when she tested the arrangement with her dagger, she had no problem maintaining her grip.

Slotting in the cable delivered a slight pulse of energy as it connected. She unplugged it again, thinking that it might be better to wait until things were about to kick off to avoid accidentally stunning herself. *That would be embarrassing.* She donned the vest next, then strapped on individual armor plates at shins, thighs, forearms, and upper arms. She fully expected both bullets and magic to be in play. Two spare magazines for the pistol went into holders on the right half of the vest, and the left side held an extra healing and energy potion.

She reclaimed the sword from Idryll and strapped it on. Her fingers touched the pommel to ensure she could draw it, and the whispers slipped into her mind again, as if the weapon was eager for battle. It was strange, not being alone in her brain. Although she'd always had that critical inner voice, this was a markedly different experience. Finally, she retrieved the other item Margrave had left for her. It was her hand-sized drone, along with a modified smartphone to control it. She lacked a good way to carry the aerial device other than in her hand, which wouldn't be optimal for most situations. *Something else to figure out.* The controller fit perfectly into the thin pocket on her left leg.

Okay. I'm ready. She turned to the others. "Staying alive is priority one. This has to be a trap, at least in part. Hopefully, we can turn it back on itself. Keeping the sheriff's people and the Ely PD alive, priority two. If we wind up with the gems, great. If we don't, that's why businesses buy insurance."

Morrigan pulled out a bunch of heavy zip ties wrapped in elastic. "I got these from the security supplies cage at Spirits. Thought they might come in handy." The big bundle was actually three smaller ones, and she handed them out. Ruby stuck hers through her belt, and the others did the same. *Better to have and not need than need and not have.*

She looked her team over and nodded. "Ready?"

They replied in tandem, "Ready."

"Okay. Let's go kick some criminals in the teeth."

CHAPTER EIGHTEEN

They exited the portal next to the trailer that served as a construction office right before dusk. Ruby released her drone and piloted it around the Casino Graveyard, holding the controller so the others could see the video feed. Nothing was happening so far, or at least nothing obvious. They agreed a pair of stacked shipping containers a little past the center would be a good spot to watch from and headed for it, maintaining the veil they'd come through under. On the way, she activated the comm to Diana Sheen. "We're here. Positioning ourselves on the double high shipping containers near the midpoint."

The woman's voice came back immediately. "Affirmative. Just arrived as well, and we're debating where to wait. Seems like the most likely entrance is from the east, so we'll deploy a decent distance in from that spot. Give them time to commit to whatever it is they're going to do before we react. I expect we'll take three different spots, and Rambo has his wings so he'll probably want to be up high somewhere."

Ruby realized she must be talking about the troll and asked, "He's not crazy enough to go up on the construction crane, is he?"

Sheen laughed. "Well, now that he's heard about it, there's no way to stop him, I'm sure."

Rath's peppy voice replied, "Up there, I'll be king of the world."

The agent gave a soft snort. "*Titanic*? Really? When did you get into romance movies?"

"Boat sinks. Plenty of action."

Sheen said, "We'll let you know when we're in position. Keep your eyes open and communicate anything you think might be even remotely useful."

Diana's connection cut off, and Ruby opened one with Alejo. The sheriff picked up after only a single ring and demanded, "Where are you?"

"Here. Also, a friendly team from an unnamed government agency is on-site as well. They'll be in black uniforms with masks, most likely."

"Got it. Not the PDA, I'm guessing."

She laughed. "I don't think those people would be any more willing to work with me than I am with them. No, someone else." She didn't want to admit to who it was, for fear that Alejo would draw the connection between Ruby and her costumed identity since Diana Sheen was connected to both. "What's the news on your end?"

"I have Ely PD with me. Decided keeping them nearby was a better choice than letting them operate as free agents. I had no other word from informants, but everything we heard before things went quiet reinforced the idea that this is the right place. If it's not, that would be really embarrassing."

"Got it. Let me know if you see or hear anything. Out." She settled in to wait for full darkness, knowing there was little else she could do. All the planning was done, and hopefully, they'd thought of everything. Idryll had stretched out on the top of the container, apparently napping, and Morrigan was crouched at the far end, keeping her eyes peeled in the direction opposite from Ruby. *She's remarkably professional and dedicated. I would've expected that from her at Spirits, so I guess I shouldn't be surprised it holds up in this situation, too. Still, it's hard to picture my little sister quite like this.* It took slightly under an hour before anything of note happened, other than some playful banter over the comms about how boring the waiting was.

The boredom vanished as if it had never existed when Demetrius connected to them. "Traffic inbound from the east. Looks like several clusters approaching from multiple vectors. I'm guessing these are the party crashers, rather than either of the principals, based on how uncoordinated they seem."

Ruby straightened and stretched, making sure her muscles were loose. Then she connected the cord to her metal knuckles. "Any sign of the people from Aces Security?"

"No. Channel's been silent for most of the day, and right now all I'm getting is the sound of a car radio. This dude's taste in music is abysmal."

"Keep an eye and an ear on it."

Kayleigh joined the channel and announced, "We have

activity around the site. I make it seven vehicles in three different groups coming from the northeast and direct east. Vehicles to the south and north may also be in play but haven't deviated toward the target location yet."

Sheen replied, "Any sign of other air traffic?"

The tech answered, "Only the drone from our ally's team. Speaking of which, Boss, she needs a callsign."

"We'll figure something out, Glam. Anyway, keep your peepers peeled. Do we have offensive capabilities?"

"Definitely. I have a self-destruct in the drone, as well as a couple of launched munitions, heat-seeking, fire-and-forget. They're small, but they'll take out another UAV fairly easily."

Ruby muttered, "Where do they get those wonderful toys?" The movie quote earned a peal of laughter from Rath. She activated her drone again and flew through the site, this time looking specifically for anything that could be a trap or other pitfall that might factor in the fight to come. Finding none, she brought the craft back and settled it on top of the shipping containers. Almost immediately afterward, both Demetrius and Kayleigh alerted them to more action. Ruby focused on his voice. "Convoy inbound. SUV-Limo-SUV. Has to be the fence and security. Coming from the north, directly toward the middle of the Graveyard."

Ruby groaned and dialed her microphone to only Idryll and Morrigan. "Naturally, they'd want to be near the middle for maximum chaos potential. From their perspective, it probably offers the most routes to escape if there's trouble. I wonder if the sellers know the bigger picture or if they're heading in blind. Maybe that's why they've been driving around all day." Their eyepieces filled with a view from Kayleigh's drone, which tracked the trio of vehicles until they were close enough to see.

They stopped in the middle of the site after reversing direction to ensure they faced in the direction of retreat. Guards spilled out of the SUVs, four from each, and created an oval perimeter around the cars. No one exited the limo. Kayleigh said, "They look human. Kevlar, rifles, sidearms. I don't see anything heavier, but they're not far from the vehicles, so there's no telling what they might be packing inside."

Sheen replied, "Enhanced scan?"

Kayleigh answered, "This isn't that kind of drone. I opted for the munitions version. Besides, the only one we have anywhere nearby with the proper sensor package is over in the place keeping an eye on the thing."

"Oh, that's right. I'd forgotten that was tonight. Okay."

Demetrius reported, "Got another car. Looks like an Escalade, a little beat up."

Morrigan observed, "Probably the seller, then."

Ruby confirmed, "Correct. I can sense the stones in that vehicle."

The meetup point was close enough for them to watch in person as the Escalade pulled up, parked, and a group of four people exited. They all held wands, revealing themselves as three wizards and a witch, and carefully examined their surroundings before walking toward the limousine. That door opened, and a tall thin man in a charcoal pinstriped business suit stepped out. He looked more like an accountant than a criminal. *Although, I guess there's probably a mass quantity of criminal accountants out there.*

Sheen warned, "Showtime," and the handshake meeting of buyer and seller was interrupted by the arrival of screeching cars, which the teams expected. Less expected was the sudden appearance of more people on foot, swarming from the debris field to the west.

Ruby breathed, "Damn. They got here before us and concealed themselves magically. Overachieving bastards."

The agent's calm voice overrode her concerns. "It's time. Everybody go."

CHAPTER NINETEEN

Diana tracked the procession of cars as they passed beneath her, waiting for the last in the convoy of seven. She wondered if they had jostled for position before entering, the different groups fighting among themselves for priority. Her rifle hung across her chest and her sentient sword, Fury, was ready over her right shoulder. She planned to strike her first blows with magic, however. She connected her comm to only her team and gave orders. "Rambo, you watch over the middle and our new friends. Croft, we'll hit the back car as soon as they stop."

Cara replied, "Affirmative," and Rath added, "Got it. Will do. Over and out."

The constant joy in his voice always brought a smile to her face. It fled as the cars screeched to a halt and scumbags piled out of them like clowns in a circus. "Going." She grabbed a pair of concussion grenades from her belt and threw one to each side of the car. After a slight pause to let them get ahead of her, she leapt into the air, aiming for the roof of the vehicle below.

Her earpieces went quiet, and her glasses darkened to protect her from the grenades' detonation, one of the better tricks Kayleigh had put into their gear. She touched down with a blast of force magic, rocking the car and allowing her to land safely. Opportunity presented itself in the form of a criminal stumbling past her position, so she lashed out with her boot, connecting with his head and putting him down in the dirt. Cries of fear and alarm mixed with shouts of anger as their opponents reacted more quickly than she would've expected.

Another pair of concussions sounded from a short distance away as Cara deployed her grenades. The distraction gave Diana a clear path to the ground, and she fired a force blast at the two closest enemies on the way down. Both called up magical shields to block the attack, and the one on the left discharged lightning at her while the one on the right tried fire. The magic deflectors mounted on her vest consumed their spells, and she whipped her sword from its sheath and brought it across at the nearest one's head, twisting it at the last instant so it was the flat of the blade that caught him on the jaw instead of the edge.

Bones shattered, and he went down howling. She rolled to the ground to avoid the next blast of flame and spun herself into a kick that landed on the second one's knee. Looking up at him, she noted that he was an elf and not a particularly attractive one. *Probably hard for him, growing up with the pretty elves.* Then the joint snapped under her assault, and he fell screaming. She popped up and looked for another target. "Glam, I need you to tag the leaders of each faction here for us, remember?"

The tech's voice came back annoyed. "Oh really, that's

what I'm supposed to be doing? Deacon's working on it, building the algorithm on-the-fly from the drone feed, and I'm looking for patterns with my Mark One eyeballs. We'll have it for you shortly, Boss. Don't get your panties in a twist. Assuming you're wearing any, you tramp."

Despite the situation, Diana couldn't help but laugh. "I'm gonna smack you so hard when I get back."

"Woo, promises, promises. What will Bryant say? Never mind, he's as much of a perv as you are. I'm sure he'd be into it."

"Maybe shut up and focus."

"On it. Data coming soon."

Ruby climbed down the side of the shipping containers under a veil, wanting to be a little nearer before she had to deal with any incoming attacks. "Morrigan, give me cover when I get close. I'm going after the gems."

As Idryll followed her down, her sister replied, "Weren't we pretty solid on the whole 'not supposed to go after the gems' thing?"

"I'm sure Diana is right that taking them out of here won't solve the problem." She dropped to the ground and skirted along the edge of the wall created by the shipping container and stacked construction debris. "But if I can get the diamonds, some might decide to chase me rather than fight. Then I'll lead them into a better position for you and Idryll to take them out."

"Ah, so you're the bait in the trap. You know, that's a good role for you. Not too demanding, doesn't require a lot of thought." Her voice cut off abruptly, then she warned, "On your left." The guard must have noticed something. Either Ruby's veil was inadequate, or the glasses he wore gave him some sort of enhanced vision. While her magic and costume were adequate to deal with thermal, visual, and aural indicators, technology was always advancing.

In any case, he was in the process of bringing his rifle to bear on her. Ruby said, "Take him." Morrigan's arrow smashed him in the chest, covering him in magical electricity and dropping him. The other guards shouted in alarm, and Ruby let her veil fall, putting all her available energy into a force blast aimed at the ones on her side of the vehicle. She traded off raw power for area of impact, and it knocked all of them staggering backward, interrupting whatever moves they were about to make. "I'm on the gems. You guys deal with the rest."

Idryll moved quickly and quietly among the rubble, staying low and counting on the strangeness of her fur to her enemies' eyes to provide the concealment she needed as she circled behind them. Ruby continued to draw their attention from the other side of the vehicles, and she noted the buyer hustling back into his car. With a grin, she adjusted her path in that direction. *Oh no, little mouse, you won't get away that easily.*

She broke into the open at the optimal distance and leapt into the air at the back of the man who was, unfortunately for him, aiming his weapon over the car's trunk at Ruby. Her mass slammed into him and bounced him off the limo, rocking the vehicle, and she landed right beside the tire. She extended her claws and stabbed them into the rubber, which immediately hissed as it deflated. She moved ahead, rising to her feet as the one firing over the hood of the car turned to bring his rifle in line.

Idryll grabbed the barrel, yanked it to the side, and punched him in the face, claws retracted. He took the impact like someone who'd experienced one before, even with her impressive strength, and responded by bringing his knee up at her stomach in a fast smash. She accepted the blow, which turned out to be sufficiently forceful to drive most of her breath away, to deliver an elbow to his skull. The force of his attack knocked her back enough that her strike wasn't final, but it dazed him.

She lurched forward, grabbed his head, and bashed it onto the car's roof. He went down, and she followed him, stabbing her claws deeply into the front tire. The vehicle listed as it deflated. Idryll tore the man's rifle from the strap that held it and used the handle as a spear, lifting and driving it into the passenger-side window. It took several smashes to get through, and she dropped quickly as the driver unloaded a pistol at her. She chuckled as an idea occurred to her, then took one of the concealment grenades, primed it, and threw it into the car. It went off a moment later, billowing smoke and forcing the occupants to tumble out of their doors. Unfortunately, they both went out the other side. *Aww, are you scared?* She crouched and circled the trunk to prepare for the next attack.

Jared Trenton sat in his SUV, several miles from the Casino Graveyard. He watched the action through the eyes of a drone hovering overhead, one of the models that flew over their headquarters at all times since the break-in. He used his encrypted comm to connect with Grentham by text message. "The costumes showed up, but there's a bunch of other people there, too. Looks like some sort of enhanced SWAT team. The police will be screeching in with sirens and lights in about a minute. Abort your entry. We'll let them fight it out. Go to Position Two and hold."

Grentham replied, "We're not finishing off the costumes?"

He laughed out loud and typed, "If there are any left alive at the end, we have the backup plan ready."

"What about the gems?"

Jared shook his head, a familiar frustration flickering through his mind. His partner's focus on money was troubling at times. "I prefer survival over cash right now, or did you forget the boss's attitude the last time we saw him? If it makes you feel better, you can always come back and round them up later, once all these people are dead."

He got a smiley face emoji in return. "Got it. Heading for Position Two."

Rath watched the fight play out below, waiting for the moment he could make the most impact. He saw his opportunity as the group of magicals appeared from nowhere. They'd apparently concealed themselves among the rubble on the far side of the spot where the trade was taking place. *Classic double-cross. Everyone should've seen that coming.* He calculated vectors and trajectories, then took an extra second to gauge the wind.

He leapt from the top of the crane, snapping out his mechanical wings to carry him past the new arrivals. Unless they looked up, he'd have a clean shot to take them from behind. Just in case, he reached down to his vest and cross-drew a pair of throwing knives, readying them for a toss. His plans changed abruptly when he saw an enemy moving in unnoticed at the tiger-woman's back.

He banked in that direction and threw the knife in his left hand at the oncoming figure. It stabbed into the man's protective vest, but the angle was all wrong, and it didn't stop him. Rath growled and dove, waiting until the last second to improve his angle while still intervening early enough to protect his ally. The next blade buried itself in his foe's shoulder near his neck, just to the inside of the vest's protection. The man's howl was audible even at his current distance, and the woman spun lightning-quick and delivered a kick to the man's head that laid him out. He pulled up sharply and collapsed the wings, landing smoothly beside her. She said, "Nice throw, Troll."

He grinned. "You owe me one, Tiger. Maybe a throwing competition sometime?" He gestured at the remaining blades on his vest.

She laughed. "Well, that's not something I'm any good at, so how about you teach me, instead?"

His grin widened. "Done deal. In return, you teach me claws. Better get back to the fight." He ran toward the newcomers he'd spotted, thinking that no one had yet claimed them. *Rath the teacher. I like the sound of that. Like Dead Poets Society, but with blades.*

Ruby finished the nearest enemy, having to resort to the pistol and anti-magic bullets to put down the single magical the fence had brought along, a wizard who had interposed himself between her and the gem sellers. They were piling back into their car, so she emptied the rest of the magazine full of incredibly expensive rounds into the vehicle's tires to disable it, wincing with every shot. *If Diana makes me start paying for these, I'm going to be screwed.* She ran all-out toward the vehicle, intent on preventing the gems from escaping.

Her blood went cold as Kayleigh announced, "Oh, hell. The Paranormal Defense Agency is on site."

CHAPTER TWENTY

Ruby heard the drone coming before it attacked, but barely. She dove out of the way as bullets stitched the car beside her. She trusted they weren't anti-magic, trusted that her bulletproof vest and personal force shield would handle any that caught her, but still, even rounds that didn't penetrate *hurt*. One of the dwarves selling the gems took advantage of the moment to shoot lightning at her, and she felt it chewing on her magical defenses.

She popped up and delivered a left cross to his temple, and it connected with a loud *crack* as the electrical knuckles detonated. He dropped immediately, the movement so abrupt she couldn't tell if he was unconscious or dead. She called up a force shield in her other hand and interposed it between her and the drone, and the continuing barrage of bullets bounced off. *So, not anti-magic. Thank heaven for small favors.* She threw fire at the drone, but it bobbed and weaved out of the way. Toggling her comm, she said to everyone, "Drones appear to be manually piloted or have really good dodging software."

Morrigan replied, "I'm on it. Take care of yourself."

Ruby grumbled inwardly at the loss of her covering fire, but it was the right move. She primed one of her electrical grenades and hurled it at the drone. She used force magic to compensate for the craft's efforts at evasion. It detonated as it struck, sending electricity arcing out to cover the device. It sputtered in place for several seconds, then plummeted to the ground, smoking. "Electricity is effective against the PDA drones."

She turned off her microphone and, after checking to be sure no more of the killer aerial vehicles were homing in on her, threw a blast of force at the car windows, shattering them.

***

Morrigan nocked and loosed arrows as fast as she could, calmly shifting from target to target as they presented themselves. Her second magical lightning arrow struck a glancing blow on one of the drones but was still enough to send it out of control. She didn't check it off her target list but moved it down to the bottom. Next up was a knockout gas arrow into a pair of the buyer's guards who had taken cover together. An explosive arrow followed, taking out a drone headed toward Idryll's position.

She cringed back as gunfire spattered the side of the container she stood on. *Apparently, they've noticed me. Unfortunate.* She cast a veil and moved to the other end, then stayed frozen until the shooter was distracted by someone closer. Then she fired what she thought of as her "screamer" at his position, the burst of light and sound jangling his nerves and sending him stumbling out of cover so her razor arrow could take him in the shoulder. She'd aimed center mass but couldn't complain about the target she'd hit.

Boots slammed on the container behind her, and she spun to find a Kilomea a dozen feet away. She pulled out an explosive arrow and launched it at him, but he whipped up an ax and knocked it out of the air. He held one of the wicked-looking weapons with a bladed front and pointed back in each hand and grinned as he twirled them. "Let's see how tough you are when you're not shooting unaware victims at a distance."

Morrigan nodded acknowledgment and hit the button to retract her bow, slipping it into the holder on her left leg when the transformation was complete. He waited, seemingly comfortable allowing her to prepare herself. She drew her daggers, gave them a quick spin in imitation of his move, and set her feet. "Let's go, big boy."

He moved forward at a measured pace, not committing to any particular action, and she advanced to meet him. His muscles were sufficient to make wielding the heavy axes seem no more challenging than her using her daggers. He brought them across in quick, brutal chops, seeming less interested in ending the battle than in inflicting minor damages that would add up. *Sadist.*

She evaded some, deflected others with her blades, and back-stepped when he tried to circle to put the edge of the container behind her. *Now, now, none of that.* She had options, including loosing her magic or using one of the grenades on her belt, but fighting him with her daggers somehow felt right. *After all, if we can't be civilized murderers, why even bother?* She slid in and fell to her knees, stabbing both her knives in at his thighs. He slashed down at her, but the move had been a feint to get inside his guard. She popped up inches away from him, ramming a knee up into his groin only to receive a leg full of pain as it impacted something metal.

He laughed and smashed his forehead down at her, connecting with the top of her head because of the height difference. Morrigan staggered in a retreat as sparkles filled her vision and narrowly avoided the first ax chop that came down at her. A quick dodge saved her from the forehand stroke of the other one, but he quickly whipped it in reverse and the point caught her in the upper left arm, stabbing deep into the muscle. She screamed and dropped her blades, hurling a force blast at him with all the magic she could reflexively muster. It was sufficient to knock him back three feet, but her brain was too disjointed to pull enough power to do more. She tossed one of Margrave's concealment grenades at her feet and stumbled backward, looking over her shoulder to find the edge while her good hand scrabbled at her waist for her healing potion.

When the smoke cleared, her arm was on the mend, but not yet useful. The blow to her head had healed, but the blow to her pride had not. She drew the pistol from her holster in a fit of anger and pulled the trigger three times, putting anti-magic rounds into his chest. He staggered backward, dropping one of his axes to *clang* on the metal surface, and tumbled off the back of the container. She sank down to a knee and switched out the magazine for a full one while she waited for her arm to heal.

Cara's glasses highlighted one of the men in front of her as Kayleigh said, "I've marked the leaders for you." A trio of guards protected him, all elves. She took out the first with a burst from her rifle, cutting his legs out from underneath him thanks to the luxury of time to aim. She followed it with a concussion grenade, then ran in under cover of its sound and fury. A car door that the elf magically ripped off its hinges and put in the way intercepted her next series of shots.

She shouted, "Impressive, but not big enough." Her follow-up barrage struck him in the feet, and when he released the shield in shock, she shot him in the chest. The next foe lifted his hands, and she reflexively dropped the rifle and conjured a force shield to protect against whatever he was going to throw at her. Only a moment of crystal intuition allowed her to dive forward and avoid the piece of concrete he summoned from behind her, dodging a nasty blow to the head that probably would've killed her if she hadn't moved.

She rolled up with a growl and stabbed both empty hands at him. Darts of fire leapt from each of her fingers and curved in at his face. He blocked about half but wasn't fast enough to catch them all and went down screaming from the burns. Then it was only her and the leader. The man calmly pulled the trigger on the shotgun he'd been concealing behind the guard. She threw herself onto her back to avoid the rounds and called up a large force shield to protect against any further shots.

From her prone position, she pulled her pistol and shot

at him, but the elf with the wounded face hurled himself into the path of her bullets. One scored a glancing blow on the leader, and the others buried themselves in the unfortunate magical's chest. She climbed to her feet warily under the protection of the shield, and another duo of bodyguards joined the fight long enough to send suppressing fire her way and pull their boss back to their vehicle. She activated her comm and reported, "Group one down."

Kayleigh chimed in, "Only four more to go."

She frowned. "Four? We had three incoming, and they've already taken down the buyer and seller. Who's the extra?"

"Rambo found them. Bunch of assorted magicals hiding among the debris."

Cara shook her head and cursed. "Boss can handle the rest of these. Vector me in to another bunch."

CHAPTER TWENTY-ONE

Rath's three-foot size provided a distinct advantage as he positioned himself to deal with the onrushing criminals. They were focused on the cars ahead of them, on winning the prize of the gems, he supposed and had no attention to spare for the small troll working his way around behind them. No attention to spare, that is, until the nearest discovered a throwing knife in his calf that caused him to stumble and fall in a sprawling roll.

Rath charged forward, now heedless of being spotted, and threw blades as fast as he could pull them. Two more went down, one of which would likely find himself in trouble if he didn't get medical attention quickly, and for the other, a woman, her head striking the ground probably did more damage than the knife in her shoulder did. He swapped to batons as he neared his targets and dodged out of the way of a blast of lightning that tried to catch him. That foe could wait since later in the battle it might benefit the troll to have someone throwing electricity at him to recharge his batons.

He angled toward a dwarf who had stopped his rush to the cars, turned to face him, and pulled out a lead pipe. That enemy grew a shade paler when Rath flicked his batons out to full extension. His foe interposed the pipe into the path of his first strike. He even deflected the second, but the third and fourth easily caught him on the shin and shoulder. A stab in the middle of his chest with both weapons finished the sequence. The first four blows generated small sparks, but the last discharged a sizeable blast that knocked the dwarf from his feet. Rath looked up and realized a couple more enemies had noticed him, a Kilomea with a nail-studded baseball bat and another dwarf carrying a pistol.

Rath shouted, "No guns," and fired his harpoon at the latter foe. It struck true, thanks to the targeting reticule in his goggles, bisecting the man's wrist and causing him to drop the gun. He bent to retrieve it with his other hand, and Rath shook his head in grudging admiration for his enemy's dogged persistence. He veered away from the Kilomea and ran up to the dwarf, launching a flurry of blows with the stun batons that put him out of the fight.

The move allowed the giant creature to catch up to him, and Rath took a kick to his protective vest that lifted him and hurled him through the air in a low arc. Without the impact protection, things inside him probably would've broken. He was already shifting before he landed. His vest split along its Velcro straps and fell away as he grew, as did his weapons belt. At his full seven-foot-plus size, with his purple hair standing up in spikes, he knew he appeared impressive and fearsome to most. The Kilomea, clearly not impressed, grinned and waved his baseball bat. "Nice trick. I'm going to smash you down to size."

Rath replied, "You have only one weapon. I have two." They closed at a dash and engaged in a sequence of strikes and parries, testing each other. His opponent broke the pattern with a kick at Rath's knee, and he jumped in the air into a somersault over his foe to avoid it. As soon as he landed, he kicked backward, connecting with the creature's thigh and knocking him away. Rath spun, leading with the baton, but the Kilomea was smart enough to get low to evade the blow. That didn't save him from the second baton, which Rath stabbed into the small of his back and held in place as it hissed and snapped.

His enemy growled and spun to bring the baseball bat around in a move that would've surely beheaded Rath if he hadn't compensated. He was already in motion, diving to the side in a roll. He rose and whipped a weapon at his opponent's head, forcing him to block, then rammed the tip of his other baton into the Kilomea's groin. This time the snaps and cracks were rewarded with shouts of pain, and while he was distracted, Rath pulled back and delivered a punch to his face with the shock glove. The last dose of electricity overwhelmed him, and the giant creature fell to the ground.

Rath shook his head at the figure below. "Who brings a baseball bat to a stun weapon fight? Honestly." He picked up his gear and loped in Ruby's direction after knocking out the couple who were bold enough to remain and fight him.

Idryll decided things were too chaotic to rely on her current body. She removed her mask and clipped it to her extendable belt, then released her magic and shifted into her tiger form. Her vision became sharper, her nose much more so, and every step flexed the wicked claws on hands and feet. She moved quietly, staying low to the ground, heading for the men who had escaped out the far side of the limousine. She peered around the corner and discovered the thin man in the suit was first in line. He was about to have a very bad day.

She raced ahead and whipped out a claw as she dashed past him, slicing through his shoe, sock, and the tendon in his heel in a swift move, causing him to fall to his knees while gagging in pain. The noise alerted the second man, who turned in time to see a tiger flying toward him in midair. She retracted her claws before the impact, the momentum and mass of her hurtling body enough to slam him down to the ground. Bones crunched in a satisfying manner as she landed on top of him.

Her moment of satisfaction was ruined as a bullet plowed along her side, fired in panic by one of two guards in front of her. She idly cataloged them as belonging to the gem sellers, not that it mattered to her in the least. Her predator mode viewed any enemy as an equally viable target. She raced forward in an evasive charge, causing the shots to miss as she dodged and varied her speed. Then she was on them, slashing at the chest of the first with her claws as a distraction while she bit the arm holding down the trigger of the other man's rifle. She landed and spun, smashing her body into the one she'd clawed and knocking him from his feet while shifting her teeth to the second man's leg to yank him to the ground with his friend. She jumped on them in turn, breaking their bones as well. Ahead stood a Kilomea, and a slow grin spread across her face as she crouched and stalked toward the giant creature.

***

Diana ran at full tilt toward the quartet of magicals firing spells at the sheriff's cars. One vehicle was already aflame, and another had all of its tires blown out. The officers' return fire was inadequate to say the least, and she cursed at local law enforcement's lack of access to anti-magic rounds. Even though they were rare and expensive, certain things should be mandatory.

She led with a force blast at the feet of the foremost, causing him to topple as he advanced and sending the others into momentary chaos as they tried not to trip over him. She drew her sword, Fury, and used it to stab the nearest attacker through the shoulder. Her skills with the weapon were profound, and she possessed adequate knowledge of anatomy to make the wound nonlethal, as long as someone stopped the bleeding relatively quickly. *If he's smart, he'll get out of the fight and deal with that right away.*

Diana dove aside as one of the PDA drones slammed bullets at her previous location and fired back at it with a concentrated beam of shadow magic. It pierced the drone and wiped out something essential inside, judging by how it smoked and spiraled to the ground. "Idiots," she muttered. "Friendly fire is not cool."

In the moment of distraction, the other two had turned toward her. The one on the left bathed her in fire that her anti-magic deflectors drank in with a loud *crack*. Diana went for her rifle, but the other grabbed it telekinetically and ripped it away from her, the strap breaking after jerking her forward a couple of steps.

She countered by throwing out a line of shadow magic that wrapped around that elf's neck. A yank smashed him into his partner, and Diana bolted ahead to deliver a flurry of punches to each, her shock gloves blasting them into unconsciousness.

She activated her comm and quipped, "Another group down. Tell the bad guys to send more goons. This is getting boring."

Laughter sounded across the channel and Cara replied, "I'm out too."

Rath added, "Same here. Heading for the middle."

Diana said, "I'll check in with the authorities. Croft, go help Rambo."

"On it."

Jared Trenton watched the battle from the drone's perspective, shaking his head in annoyance as the tables turned against his side and the costumed freaks again managed to evade his carefully planned trap. He texted, "Bringing the Feds in was a nice move on their part. Too bad it's going to end badly for all of them. Are your people out?"

The dwarf typed back quickly, "Yeah. They started in, then decided it was too much risk for their taste. I can't argue."

Jared grinned in anticipation as he pushed the buttons.

"Excellent. I say the time to pull the trigger has arrived. You?"

"Agreed."

He pressed an icon on his phone and triumphantly crowed, "Fire in the hole, you freaks."

CHAPTER TWENTY-TWO

Ruby had her eyes on the black bag inside the car that surely contained the diamonds when the ground did its best to send her into orbit. Her brain scrambled to figure out what was going on, and words like explosion, meteor, and Armageddon passed through it. The noise was deafening, but in it, she could hear specific sounds—the creaking of metal, the rending of flesh, the screams of pain.

She reinforced the force barrier around her body, spoke the activation command for her pendant, clashed her bracelets together to create yet another shield, and slammed into something that felt like metal. As she fell toward the ground, the sound of whatever she'd hit ominously shifting overrode the other noises and filled her with alarm. She strengthened the reflexive shield she'd created at the initial explosion, just like on her first day back in Magic City at the bar in the Mist. Then everything turned dark as falling objects that came down in an endless rain pummeled her.

Idryll was in midair when the detonations went off, so she had a moment to react free of the concussive effect of the heaving earth. Dirt flew everywhere, suggesting separate traps rather than a single huge one. She touched down briefly on a car as it flipped through the air and used it as a springboard to leap toward safety. She whipped her head in both directions, looking for Ruby, and spotted her a second before a cascade of metal pipes fell on top of her. Idryll hit the ground in an all-out run, weaving and dodging as things landed all around her, her only thought the need to get to her partner.

The eruptions didn't directly reach Morrigan's high perch, and she looked around in fear as detonations occurred seemingly everywhere. Secondary explosions from damaged cars and who knew what else buried in the rubble added to the cacophony. Her weight shifted suddenly, and the creaking and shrieking of metal signaled that the structural support for the containers was compromised.

She scanned the area frantically for any option to keep herself away from the increasingly unsafe ground and blasted herself off the top with force magic as the containers fell. The unsteady launch platform sent her slightly off target, and she said a small prayer as she twisted her body around so her forearm pointed in the right direction. She released the harpoon, and it sped out toward a point midway along the arm of the crane, which was remarkably still standing tall.

It caught on the metal, and the magnet took hold. Gravity pulled at her, and she swung like a pendulum. Her sigh of relief at the safe escape vanished as the crane shifted with a sudden jolt and the sound of a snapping guy wire, listing notably to that side before starting to topple in her direction. She screamed and slammed the failsafe on the top of the launcher to release the line, leaving her free-falling. From her vantage point, it was clear the crane would land directly on her, eliminating all her alternatives.

Morrigan wrenched herself around, cast a portal a foot above the ground, and fell through it. She skidded across the floor of her bedroom to slam into the wall on the far side, releasing the magic before the crane would've followed her in. Her vision tunneled, and she knew no more.

Diana was far enough away from the explosions that they didn't affect her beyond the requirement to throw up a shield to protect the sheriff and Ely PD personnel. She had the momentary pleasure of watching the falling crane take out one of the PDA drones, then forced herself to focus. "Rambo, Croft, report in."

Cara answered, "That sucked, but I'm fine. Position near the middle."

Rath replied, "All good. Safe. Saw the tiger running toward the Mist Elf."

Diana said, "Okay. Go help. If there are any bad guys,

make sure they go down. Helping our people is top priority, assisting anyone else, a distant second." She turned to Sheriff Alejo. "We have people down. I need you to run interference if the PDA shows up. Do *not* let them in until we're clear."

The other woman nodded. "Count on it." She started yelling orders to deploy her subordinates to block the various entrances to the Casino Graveyard.

Diana reached the scene to find the tiger-woman and Rath, in his large form, pulling pieces of rebar off the pile. Cara arrived as she did, and they added their magic to the effort, helping to lift the heavy objects. They uncovered Ruby, who was delirious from pain and whose leg had bent at an unnatural angle. The troll pulled her free of danger as the rest of the rebar collapsed into the space she'd occupied, and the woman moaned pitifully.

She said, "We have no time. Cara, give us a hole. Rath, carry her. Idryll, come with us." Cara opened a portal back to the vimana, and they all fled the scene.

Ruby came to coughing and choking on the healing potion dribbling into her mouth and screamed as her right leg reassembled itself. Hands pressed her down on the bed. She catalogued everyone around her and instantly noticed her sister's absence. "Is Morrigan okay?"

Diana nodded. "We checked in. Nasty bump to the head, but she took care of it with a healing potion. She's fine but couldn't come to visit you."

Ruby frowned. "Why?"

Diana replied, "Kayleigh, play it back." Demetrius's concerned tones came into her ear. "Hey Ruby, you got this message on your phone. Hope you're okay." A harried-sounding female voice replaced him. "Ms. Achera, this is White Pine Regional. You're listed as the emergency contact for one Phineas Margrave. He's here in the hospital. You can return my call at this number or come to the ICU and announce yourself."

Ruby swung her legs off the bed and tried to stand, and strong hands grabbed her to assist. She wobbled a little as she gained her feet. "I have to go."

Diana stepped directly into her line of sight and shook her head. "No, you need to do three things first. One, take a minute and let your brain slow down. You can afford sixty seconds to get right. Second, you need a shower. You can't go in there looking like you've been in a massive fight." Ruby looked down at herself and realized the other woman was right. The explosion had torn holes in her gear, and she felt as dirty as she ever had. "Third, new clothes. Cara will take you to get cleaned up, and I'll find something for you to wear. Then we'll help you get where you need to go."

Twenty minutes later, she was clean, dressed, and no longer completely frantic. *Partially frantic, that's about all I can offer at this moment.* She'd exchanged words with her sister, who hadn't been able to get past the waiting room, then had visited the nurse's station. Now, she was finally getting to talk to the doctor. She was a competent-looking woman, probably in her fifties, a brunette with gray starting to creep in. Her eyes were sharp and seemed to give Ruby a once-over for her health before she spoke.

"Mr. Margrave is responding well. He was shot three times, once in the leg, once in the chest, and a through-and-through in the arm. We got the bullets out without too much trouble, and he's fortunate they didn't do more damage. He'll need to stay in bed for a while as his internal injuries heal. Do you know what happened to him?"

Ruby shook her head. "I have no idea. This doesn't make any sense at all. Have the police talked to him?"

"No. I'll call the detectives in now that he's conscious, but he was unable to speak until a short time ago."

"Can I see him?"

The doctor nodded. "You have ten minutes, no more. Just a warning, he might be a little loopy."

A nurse took her in, and Ruby thanked him and asked to be left alone. She stepped up next to her longtime friend and rested her hand on his shoulder. "Hey, show-off. How about you leave the hero stuff to the experts?"

His eyes fluttered open, and he coughed as he laughed. "Ow. Don't be funny. Your jokes hurt more than usual."

Relief washed over her, and she grinned. "Well, at least your brain's not any more broken than it was before this. I only have a few minutes, so tell me what happened."

He nodded. "A man showed up. Tough-looking, seemed dangerous right off the bat. I closed the door on him, and he kicked it in and demanded the armor you brought me a while back." Ruby gritted her teeth but didn't interrupt. "I handed it over. It's broken, so why not? I could tell he wasn't going to leave, so I triggered the house's defenses. He ran, but not before shooting me in the chest as he left."

She nodded. "And the arm, and the leg, if we're counting."

He gave a small snort. "Didn't notice them. Having never been shot before, I was rather focused on that novel experience."

"Don't worry. It gets easier the more you do it. How did he know the armor was there? I didn't tell anybody."

He lifted a hand, then weakly let it fall. "I contacted some people about the symbols. Never mentioned where they came from, never talked about the armor. That's all I can figure. They're trusted friends, though. There's no way they would've shared it casually." Alarm crept into his words, and he grabbed her hand. "Please make sure they're all right."

She could tell he was fading under the influence of the drugs, and she patted his hand. "If it's the guy I'm thinking of, everything suggests he has some really good infomancy on his side. I'm positive that's how he figured it out. I'll check on them, don't worry. You rest."

He was asleep before she finished, so she said goodbye at the nurse's station and marched out of the hospital filled with murderous thoughts. *Okay, you feckless scumbags. Now you've gone too damn far.*

CHAPTER TWENTY-THREE

Ruby sat on a boulder in the center of the clearing that was her Oriceran village's centerpiece. After leaving the hospital, she'd felt unmoored, with no idea where to go or what to do. Everything seemed to be closing in on her, so she fled to her native planet where at least her problems weren't quite so pressing. *Sure, the place has tried to kill me a bunch of times during the venamishas, but what's a little lethal conflict between friends?*

The sun had started to creep over the horizon a couple of minutes before, and she'd been there long enough for the nighttime cold to seep into her bones. She felt as if she had become an extension of the stone, that its solidity had fused with her skeleton and she would be part of it for the rest of her life. *At the moment, that doesn't sound so bad.* She hadn't even made an effort to change into her training gear, which might've kept her warmer than the clothes she'd obtained from Diana. *I am now a rock. Like Simon and Garfunkel, I am an island.*

Her teacher's voice didn't come as a surprise. It was

earlier than expected, but Keshalla's arrival to counsel her student was as inevitable as the dawn breaking. She said, "I don't think I've seen you in this outfit."

"Borrowed. Mine was damaged."

Her teacher sat beside her on the rock, pulled her knees to her chest, and wrapped her arms around them. "Did you win?"

She shook her head. "Nobody won that one."

"Sounds like you have a story you need to tell. Go ahead and get started."

Ruby gave her the broad strokes of the battle, identifying moments where a different choice might have made a difference in the fight's outcome. When she'd shared it all, she shrugged and sighed. "Although there were places I could have maybe improved things a little, I don't see how I could've done better overall, except by choosing not to fight. That wasn't an option. Then, while I was involved, one of my allies was attacked." She explained what happened to Margrave and finished by saying, "I know it's not my fault. He made his choices, as we all did. I still feel responsible."

Keshalla nodded. "Guilt would be inappropriate because of all the things you said. Responsibility is not. That's another choice you've made and one I respect." She slapped Ruby on the arm, startling her. "Now go in and put on some proper clothes. We need to visit the mystics."

***

Much of Ruby's angst burned off on the quick march Keshalla demanded for the ascent to the mystics' community. Nadar greeted them warmly and seemed to sense they were there for a reason. He ushered them into the main building and seated them with tea, fruit, and small rectangles of the Mist Elves' traditional trail bread. For several minutes the only sound was chewing as everyone enjoyed the repast. Finally, Nadar clapped his hands together and asked, "So, what can I do for you?"

Keshalla replied, "I think it's time you shared the rest of the prophecy with Ruby."

He nodded. "Of course."

Ruby interrupted, "Wait, now there's a defined prophecy? I thought we were connecting dots?"

Keshalla shrugged. "Get enough dots in a line, and it leads somewhere. In this case, to a prophecy."

Nadar added, "Quite a doozy of one if I might be so bold. It appears that you're destined to be the leader of the Mist Elves."

Ruby burst into laughter. "Nice joke. Now, really, what's the deal?"

He shook his head and grinned. "I would never joke about such a thing. Your completion of the second *venamisha* and your success in bonding with the sword both point to you as the next *Mirra*. No one had held that title since Kaeni was in the role."

Ruby blinked, unable to process the information for a moment. Then she asked, "So that's it, then? I'm queen?" She lifted her chin in an attempt to be aristocratic. "Very well, I want my crown, my scepter, a bevy of beautiful servants to attend to my every whim, and more of this trail bread, immediately. Chop, chop."

Keshalla and Nadar laughed, and the mystic replied,

"I'm sorry, but the last of those requests is the only one we can fulfill." He tapped gently on the table, and another mystic appeared, exchanged words with their host, and bustled off. "To answer your question, no, you're not the ruler yet. You have a great road left to travel. But now, we understand the route."

Ruby leaned back on the leather of her chair and tried to put her thoughts in order. "I don't remember Kaeni being an active ruler. I thought the title was ceremonial, or hereditary, and the power part of it had gone away long ago."

Nadar nodded and paused as the refill of snacks appeared in the hands of his brethren. "We have some records, but you are correct. She preferred not to be noticed. Ruler and leader are not the same things, you see. Kaeni made great changes during her time, but she did so by cooperating with people, using influence and agreement instead of authority. Working with the skills she had, rather than the title others had given her."

"So is that how the gig works? If so, I might not be your girl."

Keshalla laughed. "I'm afraid I have to agree. She doesn't have the personality for subtle coercion."

Nadar shook his head. "How you will lead is up to you. There's no telling what you could become."

Ruby sighed. "I'm thinking tyrant. Anyway, what's the next step?"

Keshalla smiled. "Why, another quest, of course."

A groan escaped her. "I'm afraid I don't have time right now. I'm a little busy on the other planet."

Nadar nodded serenely. "That's fine. It will be here

when you're ready. Come to us when that moment arrives. Don't wait too long though."

She asked, keeping most of the sarcasm out of her voice, "Or what, the prophecy will expire?"

The mystic shook his head and looked concerned for the first time since their arrival. "No, but *you* might before you reach your destiny."

Ruby gunned the engine on her ARCH 1 motorcycle as she sped it through the early morning streets of Magic City, wearing a slightly altered version of her true image. She'd slept for a while after returning home, then awoken at dusk filled with a need to move. She'd stopped by the liquor store to pick up a couple of bottles and carried them in her backpack.

She rolled to a stop outside the closed gate of the Desert Ghosts' garage and knocked. It opened slightly, she showed her coin with its identifying "P-23," and it retracted enough for her to ride her bike past. She parked it and found Prex sitting in a circle of lawn chairs surrounding a bonfire built on an old truck tire rim. He patted the empty chair beside him. "Welcome, probie. I wondered when we'd see you again."

She swung the backpack off, sat, and rooted around inside it. She extracted a bottle of expensive silver tequila and handed it over. "Yeah, I know, I'm the worst recruit ever. Maybe this will buy me a little forgiveness?"

The woman beside the dwarf snatched it out of his hands. "On behalf of all the witches here, you're forgiven."

He laughed. "She's the only witch present at the moment, so that's not as impressive as it might seem. I'm sure she's planning to share, right?"

The other woman sighed theatrically and nodded. "Yes, of course."

Ruby pulled the other items out of her bag, which included a bottle of bourbon and a stack of nested metal cups. She laid them out, cast frost upon them, and poured, filling all four. Grabbing one for herself, she gave Prex the second, and the other two were quickly claimed. She lifted hers and toasted, "To forgiveness." The others laughed, raised theirs, and everybody drank them down.

After that she only sipped, keeping her intake low, only enough to relax, not enough to lose even an ounce of restraint. The group hit her radar as friends, but she wasn't willing to count on it, not before getting to know them much better. She wound up deep in conversation with their leader and shared in broad terms that she was stressed out and floundering a little.

He nodded. "Hero stuff's hard. It's good that you want to make a difference. You know, we're always down for another adventure like last time."

She laughed. "Well, in the event I need to take down a convoy again, you're the first people I'll look for."

"I have an idea. We're headed up to the abbey in the morning after riding around town to collect donations. How about you come with? You have an empty backpack, and it's a way to do some good that doesn't require you to put yourself in danger."

She nodded with a grin. "Will it get me closer to becoming a full member?"

He laughed. "You're still working off the forgiveness."

"Fair enough."

They stayed up all night, drinking and talking. In the morning, everyone participating in the ride drank healing potions to clear any lingering inebriation. The decision impressed Ruby on two levels: first, they were self-aware enough to do so, and second that they thought to use the potions that way. *Have to mention this to Daphne, could be her next project. Dr. Daphne's Patented Hangover Cure.* She could picture the witch as an old-time barker selling tonic.

They mounted their bikes and wound through town, repeatedly stopping to pick up donations from houses, apartment buildings, businesses, and even the casinos. When they were fully laden, they rumbled down the road to the abbey. It was tiring carrying the boxes and bags along the long path up the hill, but the reward was a beer tasting in the abbey's giant hall, which was enjoyed equally by the folks who lived there and the bikers who were visiting.

She took Abbott Thomas aside and explained who she was, drawing the connection between the allegedly human woman he knew and this version of her. He accepted the information without comment, despite the fact that he had to be aware she'd deliberately deceived him on multiple occasions. Ruby said, "I have a friend who a bad person recently hurt. He's in the hospital, out of ICU, hanging out while he knits up. I'm worried they might come after him again. Is there any way he could convalesce here, instead?"

His head bobbed in assent. "Of course. We have a healer who works with us on a part-time basis but has previously stayed on-site at need. We can ask him to do so again."

Ruby sighed in relief. "I'll arrange to have him brought here through the receiving room later today."

The older man smiled. His long white hair was unbound and looked very much more relaxed than it did when he confined it. "Excellent. We're happy to do what we can to support you. It's a good thing you're doing, you know?"

She nodded. "For a while there, I had some doubts. But yeah, I think it is. Thank you for your help."

"Thank you for yours." Together, they returned to the happy group in the hall. Ruby's mind had cleared, and she was finally ready to relax. *For a moment or two, anyway. Then it's back to figuring out how to find Goryo and make sure he spends a lot of years in jail considering what a bad idea it is to hurt my friends.*

CHAPTER TWENTY-FOUR

Goryo stepped out of the autonomous vehicle near the rear entrance of the Mist casino. His skin was burning up, and he was exhausted, but he'd won his prize. The artifact acquired from the dwarf was now embedded in his left forearm's flesh, to all outward appearances simply a hyper-realistic tattoo. He'd been tested long ago and discovered magic lay somewhere in his lineage, although it was too weak for him to access it. The artifact changed that, and he'd already briefly experimented with the shadow powers it provided. They would prove a nasty surprise for anyone who took him for a mundane human.

The only thing that dampened his enthusiasm in the slightest was the newly arrived voice in his head, constantly urging him to use its power and further its goals, which seemed to be essentially sowing chaos. Fortunately, he'd spent a lifetime disciplining his mind and body. There was nothing his passenger could try that he couldn't handle. He'd won another victory, as well. At that moment, his armor was in the hands of an expert he'd flown in to repair it and was guaranteed to be available for the big event later that night.

First, one must set the stage properly to ensure the audience shows up. Scimitar's voice in his ear assured him she had access to all the security cameras in the facility, and she guided him unerringly toward the laundry. The key card she'd arranged was as effective on that door as it had been on the outer entrance, and he walked into the sweaty room with the attitude of someone with a legitimate reason to be there.

He snagged a uniform from a rack and continued onward, detouring into a nearby bathroom to switch outfits. When he emerged, he looked like any other member of the waitstaff. The infomancer was better than a map and guided him toward the kitchen, instructing him to pause or change direction several times to avoid guard patrols. Once inside the noisy and bustling cooking area, he secured a rolling cart and placed salads from the cooler on it, covering them with metal lids. *No one will notice their absence since there are a ton of them prepared. Anyone I meet on the way will assume they're entrées going where they belong.*

He made his way through the back corridor into the hotel section and called the service elevator with another press of his key card. It would deliver him straight to the penthouse floor, and his virtual guardian would use the resources available in the computer network to ensure he arrived without a problem. When the doors closed and the car started to rise, he broke into a smile. *Won't be long now.*

The murmur in his mind was almost gleeful at the thought.

Rayar Achera sighed. He was increasingly annoyed by the other meeting participants' seemingly obsessive focus on the subject of Gabriel Sloane. The Council had discussed the fallout of rejecting his request endlessly, and there was no need to rehash it here since many of the people present were also members of that group.

The gathering was in the nicest conference room the Mist casino had to offer, taking up one end of the hotel's top level. A long oval table filled the middle of the space. A serving buffet holding snacks and beverages occupied the wall to his left. The wall to his right was floor-to-ceiling windows that provided a beautiful view of the mountains and deserts beyond the part of Ely that held the casinos. He tapped the table gently, and the sidebar conversations fell silent. "Ladies and gentlemen, the proposal under consideration is that we consider creating a canopy over the Strip, similar to the example provided by Fremont Street in Vegas."

His son Dralen nodded and added, "It would be expensive, obviously, but the technologies to program it are already developed and easy to use. Of course, whatever they're able to accomplish down there, we can most certainly improve upon."

Nods and sounds of agreement came from around the table. Each participant wore a business suit of some kind, and most wore expensive jewelry to complement their looks. Each of the city's groups was represented, as at the Council meetings, but most had brought along additional support given the opportunity, as he had invited Dralen.

It's important that he learns the inner battles among the owners, as well. I should have brought Morrigan, too.

Jailynne Sunshi asked, "Why rely on technology at all? Instead of investing the capital to build this canopy, what if we allocated that money for hiring performers? They could put on displays of magic throughout the day, which would be far more on brand."

Rayar was one of several who nodded as they considered the idea. The mention of magic brought home to him yet again how strange it felt to be in this room, cut off from his power. Hidden at each end of the chamber was an anti-magic emitter, and the devices were always active during owners' meetings to ensure utmost secrecy. Their hosts had also assured them the room was proof against any other kind of surveillance or signals, and the lack of connection on his phone suggested it was true. Not even the hotel's Wi-Fi was accessible from inside.

Elnyier countered, "That's an ongoing expense. Would it be better to invest one time and have a reduced cost going forward? We know we have the resources to do it now, without too much extension."

The others began to debate again. Rayar sighed quietly, shifted his face into a neutral expression, and focused his attention on the words flowing by.

***

Goryo stepped out of the elevator and rolled the cart toward the conference room. When he reached the end of the service hallway and entered the short corridor that preceded his destination, a pair of hotel guards instantly accosted him. They were bulky men in dress shirts and jackets but with heavy shoes that suggested steel toes and secure lacings. *Clearly from the casino's security contractor, since they're apparently human.*

The way their hands stayed crossed over their stomachs would've been enough to warn him of guns, even if the faintly visible outlines of their shoulder holsters hadn't confirmed their presence. He put on a fake smile. "Refills."

The nearest shook his head. "Rules are no one goes in. That includes you."

He gestured at the dishes. "Seriously, man, the stuff is getting cold. I'm doing what I was told to do."

The further one took a step away from the wall from where he flanked the other side of the door and turned to face him. "We're following *our* orders, which say you don't go in there. So mosey on back to the kitchen or wherever you came from." He lowered his brow and stared hard, clearly accustomed to being able to intimidate people.

Not how I wanted this to play out, but I'm adaptable. He was aware of the anti-magic emitters in the next room and didn't trust the artifact to overcome them. In fact, he noted absently that its voice had grown quieter. *It makes sense that the suppression would affect it.* That provided additional mental focus as he stepped forward with his arms spread wide. "Look, guys." He never finished the sentence. Instead, he launched himself at the man who had attempted to stare him down and delivered a pointed-knuckle punch to his throat. The guard stumbled backward, gaping in shock as he tried and failed to draw air through his fractured windpipe.

He had to give the other one credit. He had his gun

halfway out in the time it took to deal with his partner. Goryo rammed the elbow of the arm he'd punched with backward into the man's face, missing the temple but connecting with the cheekbone and possibly fracturing it. He pivoted away, stepping out with his back foot and slamming his left hand down on his opponent's right arm, which now had the pistol free of his jacket. Goryo's other hand grabbed the gun and gave a subtle turn that broke the man's wrist. He twisted the broken joint to face in the other direction, put his finger over the guard's, and pulled the trigger as he delivered a front kick past him to clear the door to the meeting room.

Rayar had risen from his seat at the first noise outside, as had several of the others. They managed no more response than that before the door banged open at the sound of gunshots. A security person stumbled backward with another man, disconcertingly dressed in a staff uniform, repeatedly pulling the trigger of the weapon pressed against the guard's torso. After three more shots, the guard fell, and the intruder smiled. "Thank you all for gathering yourselves together in such a convenient location. Now, how about a nap?"

The gun dropped as the figure's hands went behind his back. They returned to view, holding a pair of small canisters that were already smoking as he threw them onto each end of the table. Rayar instinctively tried not to breathe, but one of his colleagues rammed him in the stomach with an elbow while trying to make her escape. He huffed his breath out, then reflexively drew another in. The gas immediately sent a wave of exhaustion through him, and a moment later he collapsed, unconscious.

Goryo watched the knockout grenades do their work as he placed a mask attached to a small canister of oxygen he'd hidden under his jacket over his face. After checking to be sure the casino owners were out, he returned to the hallway. He dragged in the other guard, who was unconscious or dead, and locked the door behind him, securing the heavy latch that might have helped keep him out if they'd been quick enough. *Not so helpful as to actively prevent my entrance, of course.*

He crossed to the anti-magic emitters and placed small charges on each power cord, then moved as far away from the explosives as he could get and pushed the remote to detonate them. Moments later a portal opened, and several people came through. The one who had cast the spell to deliver them there was a wizard he'd worked with before, a man whose skills were exemplary and whose loyalty was for sale. Fortunately, once bought he stayed true, and Goryo made sure to keep him busy so he wouldn't get second thoughts.

The wizard had tagged the artifact for tracking before the operation. When he'd reached the room, the connection would have vanished, alerting the man that his part was imminent. As the anti-magic emitters failed, that detection resumed, and the wizard brought in the men Goryo had recruited for this phase of his plan. His human hirelings spread out and dragged the unconscious casino owners through the portal. The wizard, on the other hand, stepped up next to him and handed over a heavy duffel bag, a twin to the one the magical wore on his back.

I guess that's no longer a distinction I can use since I, too, am a magical. Although, fittingly, I'm descended from the Atlanteans, one of whom created this very artifact. Maybe someday he would investigate his ancestry more fully, but for now, he had a different task. He nodded at the wizard. "Okay, one more thing to do. Let's get to the basement."

As he stepped outside the door, his earpiece reactivated and Scimitar advised, "Your path is clear to your final objective, and I'll wipe the records so there's no evidence that you left the conference room by any means other than the portal. Happy hunting."

CHAPTER TWENTY-FIVE

Sinnia Achera relentlessly paced the perimeter of her office in Spirits casino, as she'd been doing since the moment she was informed her husband and son had been kidnapped. Her daughters sat together on the room's lone couch, trying to exude a calm that Ruby was sure neither of them felt. For at least the twentieth time, her mother asked, "What do they want?"

Ruby shook her head. "Money, probably. That's the most likely answer and the simplest solution."

The older woman nodded and turned the corner to stalk along the next side of the room. "Wasn't stealing the gems enough?"

Morrigan tried to reassure her. "Could be it's a different bunch. Could be anything, Mom, but we'll figure it out. They'll get home safe."

The phone on Sinnia's desk rang unexpectedly. It was the one she'd specified should only be used for contact from the kidnappers. She picked it up, and Ruby and

Morrigan moved to stand beside her. Ruby lifted her cell to the receiver and hit record as her mother said, "Hello?"

The caller was male and seemed equal parts haughty and satisfied. "By now you know that members of your family were kidnapped. There is only one way they will return to you safely, and that is for you to follow my instructions explicitly."

Sinnia interrupted, "Why have you done this?"

The voice didn't answer, didn't change at all. *Probably a recording, going to everyone at the same time.* "If you want to secure the release of your families, you will clear the Magic City Strip by eleven this evening. No police, no pedestrians, no federal agencies, no magicals hiding under disguise." He emphasized the word magicals, and at that instant, she realized it wasn't about money. "At midnight exactly, we will trade the members of your family for the three costumed vigilantes who have been terrorizing the town."

Ruby snorted inwardly. *You mean messing with your plans, scumbag. You're the ones scaring people.* "If they are not present at the appointed time, instead of transporting your families to the Strip, we will transport them to the world in between. This will be your only warning." It clicked off, and Sinnia collapsed into a chair, tears finally overcoming her.

Ruby hit the buttons to forward the recording to Alejo, whose number she legitimately had in her civilian identity, then patted her mother on the shoulder. "Go home where our people can take care of you. I'm going to visit the sheriff. Morrigan, maybe you can join me and share information afterward?"

"You got it." They headed for the receiving room and portaled to their bunker to prepare, stopping on the way to pick up Idryll, who *definitely* couldn't be excluded from whatever was to come.

Jared took the turn to go cross-country toward the GPS coordinates he'd been given and shook his head. Although they were out in the middle of nowhere, they kept their conversation guarded. "So, the news about that kidnapping is all over the place now. I've gotten messages from a few different people."

Grentham, in the passenger seat, nodded. "Yeah, my phone's been exploding with texts." Jared felt the other man's eyes as he turned fully to face him and said deliberately, "Wonder who's behind it?"

He was sure his partner shared his certainty that Gabriel Sloane, the man they were about to meet with, was the answer to that particular question. *Being rebuffed by the casino owners clearly wasn't an insult he's prepared to bear with grace.* Out loud, he replied, "Guess we'll find out, eventually. On the news, probably." He hit the brakes and stopped the SUV a dozen feet away from the familiar limousine, under the watchful eye of a semi-circle of security people.

They clambered out, underwent the obligatory pat down, and climbed into the back of the limo. Sloane was alone there, surprisingly. He couldn't remember the last time he'd seen the man without his wife by his side. His mouth was set in a thin line, neither upset nor gleeful. *Cold probably describes it best. Really cold. And far scarier than usual because of it.*

The business-suited man nodded at their arrival. "I have jobs for you tonight." He pointed at Grentham. "You will be my bodyguard until the night's activities are over. You can use your magic or whatever to get supplies, but I expect you by my side, ready to go, within a half-hour."

Grentham looked as though he might say something in response, then clamped his jaw shut and nodded. *Good move, partner.* Sloane turned his gaze to Jared. "You will round up the assistance you require to ensure that several tractor-trailers make it to their designated locations. I don't care who you have to buy or who you have to kill. Those vehicles absolutely must be where they're supposed to be at the appointed time."

Jared replied, "Of course, Boss. If you have any more information to share, it could make our plans more effective."

His slight frown was like a warning shot. "Your constant failure has lost you the right to that information. Now, you'll do what you're told, when you're told, and that'll be the end of it. Maybe, once you rack up a lot of successes, you'll be able to move a rung up the ladder toward your previous trusted position." He stared at them for a second, then added, "Make no mistake. Failure now means death, but only after a long time of *wishing* you were dead. Now get out and get to your tasks."

They complied and walked over to the SUV. Grentham muttered, "Well, that was certainly something. Take care of yourself, and if you decide now is the time, let me in on it."

Jared nodded. He didn't think they needed to run, but

he would make sure he was ready to do so as soon as he returned to the city. "You do the same. Stay safe."

<hr>

Grentham closed the portal from the security of his shop's office and released a string of curses. Whether the fear that he was actively fighting off inspired them or his anger at the dismissive way Sloane had treated him, he didn't like the feeling or the man who'd caused it. He moved to the wall on the side of the room that faced the adjoining business and whispered a spell. The illusion he renewed daily vanished, revealing a small set of dials, and he put in the proper code. A wall section, invisible in its seamlessness, opened slightly with a small *pop*. He pulled it open and hit the switch to activate the lights.

His combat gear was inside, and he stripped down and changed into it as quickly as he could. Heavy cloth designed to stop objects from slicing through it formed the base layer, along with boots reinforced with metal in several locations. A thick leather-and-ceramic collar wrapped around his neck to protect him from strikes to the vulnerable areas it covered. A bulletproof vest was next, and a military web belt went on underneath. He slipped magazines filled with anti-magic bullets into leg pouches, one for his rifle and one for the pistol that rode at his left thigh.

He withdrew the pair of axes he'd had since he was a teenager and had used on countless occasions. The blades were honed to a razor edge and kept that way with biweekly cleanings, and he was equally proficient with them in both melee and ranged combat. They slipped into protective sheaths at his hips, the handles pointing down and back. Last on was the rifle, a military model with a grenade launcher underneath. The strap that carried it contained half a dozen rounds of multiple varieties.

He closed the closet and headed for the front of his shop. *Okay, what would be best for whatever might happen?* He chose a necklace with a moon pendant that held a shield spell, frost if he remembered correctly. Not the most powerful thing, but the best he had at the moment. He grabbed a pair of thick metal bracers and strapped them to his forearms. They would serve a dual purpose. First, they were strong enough to protect him from most handgun bullets unless someone was packing a big caliber. More importantly, their magic would activate when slammed together the right way. It generated a piercing noise that would explode the eardrums of anyone in a fifty-foot radius who hadn't protected themselves first, according to the person he'd purchased them from. *For emergencies only, in case it turns out he was lying.*

He portaled out of his office and into one of his pawn-shops. His people lurched up at his arrival, and he nodded a greeting. "I'm gonna need your help tonight, boys. Link up with this collar so you can trace it." They all touched it and concentrated to connect their magic to the item. "I'm heading out into the desert, but I want you to watch. If I don't return to the city before dawn, no worries, but I'm pretty sure I'll be here. If I am, you need to be close enough to intervene. Above all, stay hidden. No one, and I mean no one, can know you're there. Finally, if you see me spread my arms wide like I'm planning to slam my forearms together, shield yourselves."

One of them asked, "What's the deal, Boss?"

Grentham shook his head. "I wish I knew. All I can tell you for sure is that it's probably going to be big, and it's probably going to be bad. Stay on your toes, and maybe we'll all survive until morning."

Ruby and her team were in the bunker with all of their gear laid out, ready for them to put it on and jump into action. *Four hours to go. I never understood the phrase "time crawls" before this.* The surrounding room seemed empty and barren in a way it hadn't before, and her thoughts turned to Margrave, now safely ensconced in the abbey. *At least they'll take care of him, no matter what happens tonight.* She wasn't sure what the kidnappers had in mind but knew her chances of getting out of the situation alive weren't exactly blowing the roof off the likelihood scale.

Her sheathed sword lay on her lap as she sat cross-legged on the couch. Morrigan and Idryll had tried to talk to her a couple of times, but she couldn't tear herself away from her ruminations. If they were logical, contained, focused, that would be one thing. However, her brain was rambling, babbling like an idiot. With an internal sigh, she drew the weapon and hurled the scabbard to the side, then settled the blade on her thighs and sent her thoughts inward.

The beach materialized around her, with Shalia and Tyrsh standing nearby in their matching outfits. Ruby shook her head. "Not this, not now." She made an effort of will and the scene changed, becoming a virtual version of an empty Magic City Strip, with only ghostly hints of the casinos bordering the sides.

Shalia asked, "Where are we?"

"My next battleground, and possibly the place where I die."

Tyrsh said, "So you have turned to us for counsel at this moment of challenge? Highly intelligent choice. You intuitively understand what we can be."

Ruby sighed. *I'm so sick of secrets and puzzles.* "Pretend that I don't and explain it to me."

He clasped his hands behind his back with a nod. "Between us, Shalia and I have abundant experience in a multitude of things. Her approaches are more subtle, mine more martial, but both of us are equally deadly to those who would oppose us. Or our wielder."

"So counsel me, wise trapped sages."

The woman laughed, lower than she had the last time. Ruby got the impression she might've been putting on an act at their first meeting, attempting to seem less than she was. *Subtle indeed.* "Wisdom, maybe not. Experience girding for battle? Unquestionably. Let me guess. You feel afraid. Afraid for yourself, afraid for those who will enter the fray beside you, afraid for those bystanders who might be injured by your actions, or those who most definitely would be by your inaction."

Ruby grunted. "Right on the mark."

Tyrsh took up the conversation. "Somewhere inside,

you're criticizing yourself for feeling that way. As if you should be strong, should know everything about everything. Don't try to deny it. People like us always face that moment."

"Yeah. I'm aware."

Shalia said, "It's not about battling the fear, overcoming it, or denying it. Instead, you must be *with* it, accept its presence and move on. Doubtless, you've learned to do this with pain, to keep pushing regardless of what your body might feel. To even use it as fuel to push forward."

Ruby nodded. "True. But that's easy because it's me."

Tyrsh lifted a hand, palm up. "Exactly. Now you must grow, become bigger, accept this new challenge."

"The odds aren't too good."

He laughed. "Oh, how many times I have gone into battle feeling that way. You may even be correct, but it doesn't matter. You know what does?"

Keshalla had drilled her endlessly on that particular topic. "Only my actions."

Shalia replied, "Exactly. Who you are is what you do. Not what you think, not what you believe, not what you say. Your actions tell your truth."

Tyrsh asked, "Have you decided what you'll do?"

Ruby nodded. "That part's not complicated. Show up as I've been told to and fight."

The other woman shook her head. "If it were that simple, you wouldn't have come to us. There's something more."

The words jumped out of her as if they'd been itching to escape. "What if it's not a fight they want? What if the price for freeing those they've taken is the surrender of my team and I?"

Shalia clarified, "By surrender, you mean death."

Tyrsh observed, "This is a familiar conversation between us, is it not?" He didn't wait for her to respond. "So at issue is the same question. What is your life worth? Of course, this choice isn't only yours. If you do sacrifice yourself, will it save your friends? Will it save those your opponents have put in danger? Can you trust your enemies that far?"

Her doubts crystallized, and she realized that was the issue she'd been circling without addressing. "No, I don't think I can. I focus on whether I should choose to sacrifice myself, not on what would happen if I did. Of course, they won't keep their word."

Her passengers nodded as one. "Then you have your answer. You cannot trust them, so you must defeat them."

Ruby opened her eyes, taking a minute to adjust to the real world. Her voice was raspy as she announced, "We're not trading ourselves for them. We need a way to get the kidnap victims away from the scene."

Morrigan replied, "I've been thinking about that, too. Seems like it would be simple enough to have members of the families nearby under veils. They can cast portals underneath the captives' feet from a distance, and our people fall to safety, maybe on some mattresses or something."

Ruby chuckled darkly. "Taking a page from your recent experience, eh?"

The ghost of a smile fluttered across her sister's expression. "Turns out I can learn. How about that?"

"We can't pull any punches on this one. When we hit, we hit fast. If things go right and they survive to be sent to prison, great. There's no telling what other tricks they have planned though, and I'd rather not find out by losing someone we care about."

The others nodded, and Idryll replied, "Exactly what I was about to suggest."

Ruby snorted. "Of course you were. Carnivore."

Idryll bared her teeth in reply. The soft *ping* of an incoming signal startled her, then Demetrius said, "Okay. Get this. Our guy is back on the radar. All I've had for ages is the terrible music he listens to, but now he's muttering to himself. Something about trailers and parking. I think they probably switched to texting for most communication, which means they're seriously paranoid."

Morrigan interjected, "Guess Ruby will have to go on another date with him."

She responded to her sister absentmindedly. "Shut it. Tree, anything more?"

"No, I have nothing else from him."

"Okay, pass that on to Diana's team and Sheriff Alejo, please. Oh, and can you give us a flyover of the Strip?"

Clicking sounded in the background. "Coming right up."

She grabbed her mask and put it on to await the feed, noting that the others copied her action. It took about a minute before the scene sprang to life. The wide pedestrian area that ran between the hotels was deserted. She'd never seen it that way, not even once, at any time of the day or night. It was a downright spooky spectacle. The drone flew the length of it, then circled and went higher, showing what was happening at the intersections with the casino walkways. Every access had a vehicle positioned across it, marked and unmarked cars and trucks. Standing at each was at least one person with a rifle, again, some in uniforms and some unmarked, but with the bearing of police. Accompanying each was a volunteer from one of the magical families that owned the casinos, or maybe a trusted staff member. They maintained force barriers to back up the police and ensure no one got onto the Strip.

She asked, "Morrigan, can you coordinate getting the rescue in place?"

"On it." The drone swung around wildly and acquired a group of people walking down the middle of the pedestrian area between the casinos. She was concerned for a moment before she realized it was her mother and several other Council members. They strode along calmly, looking in all directions, presumably verifying that everyone met the kidnappers' demands. She checked her watch and saw that the deadline for having it cleared was ten minutes away. She breathed, "Good work, Mom," then removed the mask.

Her sister coughed, and Ruby shifted her attention in that direction. Morrigan was rolling an arrow between her fingers, staring at the razor point on the end. She asked, "Do you think we'll get them back?"

She gave a slight shrug, more a nervous tic than a real movement. "I hope so. There's nothing to be gained by killing them, but it's not as if we're dealing with rational individuals here. All we need is for them to honor the deal long enough for us to snatch our people away."

Her sister gave a vacant nod. "They?"

"Goryo, for sure. Going after the armor has to be part of this. It's too much of a coincidence otherwise. I'm not sure who else."

"The Aces Security guys." She said it as a statement, not a question.

Ruby nodded. "Probably. Still, there's someone unknown behind them, pulling their strings, and that's the person or people I'm most worried about."

Morrigan lifted the arrow. "I have a solution for that. A quiver full of them, in fact. Just show me who to shoot."

She had no answer for that, so she remained silent. When the clock hit eleven-twenty, they started donning their gear by unspoken agreement. At eleven-fifty, Ruby said, "I love you both. Stay alive, no matter what. I couldn't continue if I lost either of you."

She locked her feelings down and pushed them as far into the background of her mind as they could go. "Let's get moving."

CHAPTER TWENTY-SEVEN

Goryo moved through the dwarf's portal first, stepping out of its path and turning a complete circle to ensure no nasty surprises were present. He waved at the others, and Gabriel Sloane and Grentham came through alongside a pair of wizards with raised wands. Goryo took a step forward and gave a slight bow toward the trio of costumed figures that awaited him. "I see you've chosen to accept my invitation."

The one with the sword and the dragon's face, standing farthest to his right, nodded. "Show us your hostages, and we'll talk."

He muttered, "Do it," to the radio inside his armor's helmet that connected him to Sloane and the dwarf. The former called, "Bring them," and the wizards marched the captives through the portal. Their hands were bound behind them, and each had tape over their mouth. Hoods would have been his preferred option, but then they wouldn't have been recognizable. When all were present, and the rift was gone, Goryo said, "A simple trade. You for them. Agreed?"

The woman turned to look at her companions before nodding again. "Agreed."

Sloane barked, "Change of plan. Kill them." Goryo twisted and drew his pistol in a single motion, putting anti-magic bullets into the foreheads of both wizards, who had only begun to move. He kept the weapon trained on the dwarf and said coldly, "No changing the deal. Once given, a promise is binding. If you want to find them and kill them later, that's your prerogative. Today, we will honor our word."

Sloane stared daggers at him through the eyeholes in his mask. "Word of this lack of obedience will get around."

He shrugged. "The ones who are worthy of my business will understand. Stand down." Sloane grumbled and moved away, the dwarf following him. Goryo turned to the costumed people. "Lay down your arms and come forward."

Ruby considered the request one final time and discovered she still agreed with Tyrsh and Shalia. *Sacrificing myself accomplishes nothing. Sometimes, you have to blow things up.* She laughed inwardly. *Especially if it's a door. Hope you're thinking good thoughts about me right now, Keshalla.* She replied, "I don't think we will." That was the signal for their helpers, and a portal instantly replaced the ground beneath the captives' feet. They were gone in the blink of an eye, and the hole closed before anyone could pursue.

The armored man across from them laughed. "Well played. I had no doubt this would occur—that we would once again share a battlefield. Given the outcome the first time we met, I'm eager for a rematch."

Ruby grinned, appreciating his style even if he was an evil bastard. "Then bring it on, scumbag." She circled to her left, Idryll stayed in position, and Morrigan moved to the right. They each had their assigned responsibilities, and hers was exclusively to deal with the man who had hurt Margrave. She sized him up as she closed, searching for any areas of vulnerability. A frown appeared as she thought back to their prior meeting and realized there was a significant difference.

She triggered the comm. "His armor is different this time. Left arm is covered only to the elbow. Might be an opportunity, might be a trap. Keep an eye on it." He raced at her while drawing his sword with a ringing chime. She matched him, knowing the magic-resistant armor would dissolve any power she threw at it and not wanting to use any of her toys until she thought they'd make a difference. *Can't waste any advantage here.* His blade slashed down at her head, and she brought hers up in a block that deflected it to her right. She drew and stabbed her dagger in a single move, but it scraped off his armor without penetrating. *Damn, it's as solid as I remembered.*

They clashed three more times, his weapon gouging a seam in her protective vest and hers almost catching that bare arm before his subtle shift moved it out of the way. Plans ran through her mind as they fought, her body taking care of the blocking and striking while she worked on identifying a useful strategy. She'd lost track of time in the haze of battle but trusted Morrigan was moving into position to do her part. She noted in passing that he had an extra bandolier across his chest in addition to the strap that secured the scabbard on his back. Several canisters and what looked like darts filled it. *Wonder if Margrave had those knockout darts made, and the bastard stole them. He didn't mention it, though, so probably not.*

They crossed swords another trio of times. She managed a slice across the top of his knuckles, the welling blood a little reward. He suddenly turned and dashed away several steps, making a strange twisting motion with his body. When he spun to face her, his left hand gripped the shotgun that he must've attached to the back of the bandolier. She dove aside as he pulled the trigger, not willing to trust her magical defenses against this man, not after he'd drilled her full of anti-magic rounds the first time they'd fought.

Morrigan moved to her right, keeping one eye on Ruby's battle and the other on the dwarf and the person he was apparently protecting. She presumed it was a dwarf, anyway, based on his height. *Might be a troll, but doesn't move like one, at least not the one I've met. Less bouncing, more stomping.* He cast a shimmering wall to separate her from him and his boss, and she gave him a nod. *Stay right there buddy. I'll get to you afterward.*

She reached back and selected an arrow by touch, coming out with a gas arrow. *Maybe if I'm lucky, Ruby's opponent's armor won't block this.* She drew and waited for the perfect moment, knowing Ruby would eventually move him into position for her to strike. Her sister dove out of the way as a loud blast went off, and Morrigan let go of the string without thinking. The projectile shot true, slamming into his shoulder and detonating to spread a gas cloud all over him.

She watched, hoping he would fall, and reached back for another arrow. She chose explosive, one of the technology-based arrows the agents had provided. He dropped the shotgun, which hung from a strap, and grabbed something on his chest. The arrow sped toward him in the same moment he threw a canister at her. She sent a blast of force at it to deflect it out of line and called up a shield to protect herself from the now-more-distant detonation. *Too bad I didn't have enough time to marshal some energy and throw it back in his face.*

Her arrow hit the concrete at his feet and blasted him backward, his magic armor not proof against a very material-world concussion. She chuckled, then the grenade detonated. Her entire side erupted in flame as shrapnel ripped into it, passing heedlessly through her protection without even slowing. Only the distance she'd knocked it away saved her from being shredded. She collapsed to the ground, clawing at her healing potion and trying to maintain a hastily summoned shield to separate her from any attempt by the dwarf or his friend to take advantage of the situation.

Idryll's first instinct was to help Morrigan or at least charge the dwarf and the human to keep them away from her fallen partner. *No, I have to trust her to take care of herself.* Her assignment was to wait for the instant the armored man was fully distracted, then get close and do her thing. The armor had turned her claws aside before, but mass was mass and strength was strength. It didn't matter to her if his bones broke inside the armor or she ripped them out through his flesh, as long as they were out of commission.

Their foe being prone from the arrow's detonation fit the criteria. She charged forward with a roar that always sounded strange coming from her two-legged form and leapt into the air, intending to come down on his legs, hoping the explosion had done some damage to his magical protection. She twisted violently aside as he whipped something at her, a dart that turned into a bolt of flame as it traveled toward her.

It slashed across her face, burning into the flesh of her cheek, and by the time she landed, she was in her four-footed tiger form, having lost only a second in the transition and adjustment. He scrambled backward, going for another one of the darts, but she jumped over him, digging her front claws into the join of his shoulders and neck and flipping him over with the intent of ripping his skull from his body. She yelled in pain as the armor's magic tore into her, her very nature anathema to it, but his head came off.

She tumbled, giddy with success until she realized her hands only held his helmet. The man himself was back on his feet with a grenade in each hand. He threw one at Ruby and another at her, then grabbed the gun dangling from the strap at his side.

Grentham had wanted to take advantage of the archer's fall, but the boss had refused his request. *Getting really tired of this bastard telling me what to do.* He forced calm into his voice. "Do you have any orders, then?"

Sloane's smile was apparent in his tone. "No, wait. The best surprise is about to arrive. I'm not sure if you're aware of this, but the Paranormal Defense Agency, for all their good intentions, doesn't have particularly strong security. Does it, Scimitar?"

A new voice, female and computer-modulated, joined the channel. "Nothing that I couldn't break with five minutes of effort. Are the drones a go?"

Sloane laughed. "Oh yes. The drones are a go."

CHAPTER TWENTY-EIGHT

Morrigan forced herself to her feet as the healing potion she'd consumed did its work, filling her side with even more agony as it pushed the shrapnel out. She muttered curses against the pain as she retrieved her bow, single-mindedly looking for the man who'd hurt her. She spotted him across the Strip, his helmet off and an angry look on his face.

It required no thought to draw and fire a razor arrow aimed squarely at his head. She expelled additional curses as the projectile missed, his move to reengage with Ruby taking him out of line. Then a loud buzzing from above caught her attention as a trio of drones bore in on her, spitting bullets. She called up a force shield anchored to her left arm and crouched behind it, praying the drones carried ordinary rounds. At the rate they were coming, it would've cost a mint to arm them, if not.

Their barrage deflected from the shield, the impacts feeding back into Morrigan's arm as the faintest echo of the pain she'd experienced. The drones split, one continuing forward and two moving to encircle her. She broke into a run, heading toward the dwarf and the man he was protecting, figuring that would at least shield her from one angle if they felt the need to act in defense against the PDA. She tripped and rolled, then drew and came up shooting, launching an explosive arrow at the nearest drone. It struck true, blasting off two of the thing's fans, and the aircraft spiraled out of control in the direction of the casinos. *Hope someone is watching out for property damage.*

She lurched back into motion as bullets traced a line toward her, courtesy of another of the drones making a strafing run. She called, "Drones suck. Mine don't have anti-magic rounds, but they have a lot of the regular kind."

Kayleigh's voice entered the conversation and urged, "Keep moving. Help is on the way." Morrigan followed the advice, taking a circuitous route toward the nearest enemies to avoid spooking them. *Sorry, Ruby. You're on your own for a while.*

Ruby caught pellets from the shotgun in her leg, and when she rolled back to her feet, her movement included a significant limp. Spotting the inbound grenade, she reached out with a burst of force magic, knocking it as far away from the combat areas as she could. She'd seen the one he'd hurled at Morrigan and wanted no part of it.

It required willpower to quash her desire to check on her sister and move toward Goryo instead. He matched her motion as he raised the shotgun to point it at her, but then three drones swooped in at her, bullets leading. Reflex took over, and she blasted force magic into the ground to lift her high into the air. She discharged electricity at the nearest on her way up, causing it to pause and hover, and a crazy, stupid idea occurred to her.

She twisted her body to adjust her trajectory and landed on top of it. It was about the size of a large chair but not designed to hold her weight. The fans gave a struggling *whir*, then flamed out, and she used another blast of force magic at the ground to propel her in a shallow arc toward the next closest drone. It flew to meet her as if eager for the battle, and she summoned a force shield on her arm to intercept the barrage of bullets it sent her way, adjusting the angle in flight as the drone tipped slightly upward, seeking her head.

Whatever other defenses it had, proximity alarms weren't among them. She got close enough to slash her sword down through it, and the magically keen blade bisected the device. It fell a few feet ahead of her, and hers plummeted toward the ground. She landed on another blast of force magic, cushioning the impact, then snatched one of the electrical grenades from her belt and hurled it at the last of the trio. Force magic corrected its trajectory, and seconds later the drone was down. *I'm getting good at this. Unfortunately.*

The sequence had given her opponent time to close, and she frantically grabbed the concealment grenade, throwing it and moving right before he fired the gun. Pellets slammed into the back of her Kevlar vest, feeling like a hundred sharp punches. None made it through to her flesh though, and she said a quiet thank you as she slipped under a veil and circled toward her target.

***

After hurtling away from the grenade he'd thrown at her, Idryll had stalked her quarry from behind, taking advantage of his intense focus on Ruby. He hadn't taken his eyes off the other woman, making it easy to creep in with him unaware of her presence. She needed to make the attack good, this time ripping his head off for sure before any more nasty tricks came into play. She accelerated and jumped.

Something must've given her away, perhaps her claws on the concrete because he twisted toward her and thrust out his left arm. *Perfect, I'll bite it off.* Instead, tentacles shot from it, long, slender limbs composed of shadow magic. They grabbed her in midair and slammed her to the ground, leaving her as stunned as if she'd fallen from ten times that height. Then, worse, they began to constrict.

***

Morrigan was about a dozen feet away from the pair when the dwarf spotted her and called up another force shield. She was surprised he wasn't mixing it up, but clearly his sole objective was to run interference for the other man. *Which makes that guy a high-value target.* She considered the angles and fired an arrow in a tall arc, hoping to land the knockout gas at their feet by shooting it over the barrier.

As it turned out, the dwarf was too cagey for that

because her projectile bounced off an invisible section of the protective surface over their heads. His masked head nodded, and she returned the gesture. *Don't worry. I'll come up with a plan to deal with you. For now, how about this?* She pulled her screamer, the arrow version of a concussion grenade, and shot it at the armored figure with the tentacles coming out of his arm. *Wait, tentacles? What the hell?*

<hr>

Idryll spotted the projectile on its approach and waited a beat until it was close. Right before it struck, she shifted into her house cat form, leaving her belt and mask behind as she scampered away from the tentacles, which collapsed around the spot she'd vacated. She was sure they were reaching for her, was already dodging out of the way, but when the arrow hit, it exploded with sound and noise sufficient to make her head ring. Her most devout hope was that it did worse to its intended target.

She gave up on trying to stalk the man and instead ran toward Ruby, who had appeared suddenly after the arrow's activation, staggering backward from its effects. It only took a few steps before she was back in her large four-legged form, and only a few more before she arrived. Her partner grinned as Idryll padded up next to her. "Welcome to the party. Watch out for him throwing things. He has some stuff that sucks."

<hr>

The tiger nodded, which was an amusing sight in itself. Ruby called, "Hey, chucklehead. How about we go back to the swords and quit this dancing around?"

He lowered the shotgun and threw it aside. Drawing his sword, he gripped it in two hands, a different fighting style than he'd used before. He flowed smoothly toward her, and Idryll moved left while she moved right, ready to put her steel against his. She struck at his head, and he blocked it with his blade. She went low, and he stopped it with a booted foot. She growled, "That damn armor sucks, and his head is too easy a target to defend. Morrigan, can you shoot him?"

Her sister replied, "Afraid not. I'm dodging another set of drones over here."

Kayleigh interjected, "We'll take care of you in a second. That tip you gave earlier about the trailers finally percolated through our systems to something useful. We have a pair of threes: three eighteen-wheelers from a delivery service parked by three casinos. Deacon was able to hack into the company and discover they were stolen."

Ruby's blood ran cold. "Explosives, you think?"

The tech replied, "It's what I'd do. Don't worry, though. We're parking signal jammer drones on top of all three. Unless they have some amazing skills, magic, and technology, they're not going to get through our blocking. Trust me on this. We've tried to break it every way we know how."

So that's the twist, Ruby thought. *Try to kill the casino owners, try to kill us, and if things go wrong, blow up the casinos. Pretty nasty.* "I'm sure they've already evacuated the customers, but we need to make sure they get staff out.

Demetrius, call the casino master number I gave you and tell them to initiate a Priority Diamond action. Everyone will know what you mean, and helping to pass the word is part of the protocol."

Her boyfriend replied, "On it." She heard the worry in his voice and realized suddenly that some of it might be about her. *Can't be fun sitting back and listening to all this nonsense, I suppose. Maybe I need to pony up and take him on a date instead of the other way around.*

Idryll's feint at their shared target focused her mind on the moment, and she ran toward him. She sheathed her sword, deciding it was time to try something different given her spectacular lack of success thus far. She summoned shields on both arms and flexed the left hand with the metal knuckles attached. He dodged away from the tiger, providing an opening for her to get close.

She punched at him, sure that it would be a knockout, but he leapt into the air so her blow slammed into his armor instead. A finger broke, and she howled, more in annoyance than actual pain. Still, he was off his feet, if only for an instant, and that was something she could work with. She threw herself into him, leading with her shoulder and knocking him off-balance. Idryll raced in from the side and smashed into him, taking him to the ground. A shadow shield wrapped around him before he hit, preventing the tiger from getting in to do more damage, and he stood under its protection.

Ruby decided she had endured more than enough of the smug look on his face, and if she was going to have broken bones, he deserved to receive some pain, too. She reached down with her right hand and snagged a throwing knife from her boot. She threw it as hard as she could, and it stabbed into the bare flesh of his left arm. He howled, an unreasonable amount of anger flowing from him, and she suddenly saw the whole picture in perfect clarity. "Holy hell. He has an artifact inside him."

Demetrius snapped, "What?" Morrigan replied, "That explains the tentacles," and Kayleigh growled, "Damn, be careful. Those things suck."

Ruby didn't need to be told twice, but she had no decent options. As he dropped the shield, she closed in again. *If I can hit him with a good left hook, it's nighty-night for scumbag.*

Morrigan stopped moving as the hooded man the dwarf was defending pulled a device from his pocket and held it up for her to see. It looked like a small flashlight with a big red button on the top that flashed alarmingly. She said, "I hope you've got those trucks locked down. He's holding a detonator of some kind in his hand."

Kayleigh's urgent voice asked, "Is it a dead man's switch?"

"What?"

The tech let out an exasperated sigh. "Is he currently pressing it? If he is, it probably goes off when he lets go. If he's not, it's pushing the button that does it."

"Okay, no, not pushing it."

"Good. The last jammer will be in place in fourteen seconds. No sudden movements."

She snorted inwardly. "Right, sure." She looked at Ruby

and Goryo, who were close together, and realized she had no chance to hit him without hitting her sister, too. Still, maybe she had a way to even the odds a little. As she pulled out the sonic distortion arrow and fitted it to the string, she warned, "Incoming, Ruby. Try not to fall." Then, before she allowed herself to reconsider, the arrow sprang from the bow and raced toward its target.

CHAPTER TWENTY-NINE

Ruby collapsed under the sonic shock of Morrigan's arrow, which had hit the ground between her and Goryo. She struggled to get back to her feet faster than her opponent when suddenly the attack on her inner ear vanished. He looked satisfied about something as he popped up and pulled his sword from its sheath. He swung at her, a wicked horizontal chop from the left, and she reached for force magic to coat her arm to block.

It wasn't there. Her mind had enough time to panic and send her tumbling out of the way before the blade chopped her in two, but she took a slash along her left arm that burned like acid. Figuring that if her shield didn't work, his probably wouldn't either, she yanked out her pistol and pulled the trigger convulsively, emptying the magazine in a flurry of shots. He crouched, covered his head with his arms, and let the armor absorb the impacts. Then he was up and rushing toward her again, and all she could do was charge at him with a scream, hoping she could get one hand or the other close enough to his unprotected face to end the fight.

As Kayleigh announced, "Drones are down. You can take him out," something changed with the dwarf and his boss. The shield fell, the dwarf pointed his weapon at her, and a grenade shot out of the tube under the barrel. Morrigan used force power to send the projectile back at him. His instinctive reaction was to do the same, and it flew off to explode where it couldn't hurt anyone. She pulled an arrow and launched it, and he batted it out of the air with magic. She tried it again, and he repeated the defense.

He dropped the rifle and pulled a pistol, allowing him to cast with one hand and attack with the other. She bolted, cursing the lack of cover in the area as she ran a weaving path, waiting for the inevitable moment that a bullet caught her. When it happened, it was in the form of a triple punch in the back that sent her sprawling, but the rounds didn't get through the armored vest.

Morrigan jumped up with a growl and dispatched a wash of fire at him, but he called up a shield to deflect it. She had no doubt she could take him in a different situation, where she could focus exclusively on him, but her eyes kept drifting to the man with the detonator and the one mixing it up with Ruby and Idryll. She ran to her right, doing her best to make the dwarf move so he'd be back-to-back with his boss. Then she sent in a gas arrow intended as a distraction. It hit the ground between them, and while the dwarf used his magic to push the vapors away, she loosed her last razor arrow at his face.

Ruby swung at Goryo, and he blocked her arm with his armored forearm, then slashed at her head with his sword. She ducked under it, guiding his wrist up and away, then reflexively punched his exposed ribs. She pulled the blow as soon as she remembered he was wearing armor and she wasn't, but when the knuckles struck they snapped with a loud shock. The noise startled him, and that gave her the instant of vulnerability she needed.

Idryll had moved around behind him, and Ruby jumped and delivered a two-footed kick to his chest. She flew backward to sprawl on the ground, but so did he, right over the top of the tiger that had read her move and driven herself at the back of his legs. He landed hard, and Idryll twisted, leapt into the air, and descended on him with all her weight, the loud *crack* indicating the blow had compromised his chest armor.

Ruby dashed to his side and encased his left lower arm in a force shield on the way, ready to chop the limb off with her sword if her magic failed again. It confined the tentacles that tried to lash out and gut the tiger. He'd lost his weapon during the fall, and his free hand grabbed a grenade on his bandolier. Idryll dove off and captured his hand in her fangs, yanking his arm to the side hard enough to make the chest crack a little more. Ruby fired lightning into the damaged portion, and he stiffened and shook. She finally put him out with the punch to the face she'd been trying to land, discharging the remaining stun power and overloading his nervous system.

She fell to her knees, panting from the blood loss caused by her wounded arm, and popped open her other healing potion. "For the love of all that's holy, please make sure this bastard doesn't get back up, even if you have to tear his arm off to do it."

Idryll's grin was visible even with Goryo's forearm trapped between her fangs.

The arrow whizzed across, and only a last-second dodge kept the dwarf from being impaled. While the bolt missed him, it didn't miss the other person she was aiming at and slammed deep into the back of the man he was supposed to protect. He ripped off his mask, seeming to gasp for air as he turned reflexively to see where the grievous injury had come from, and she recognized him immediately: Gabriel Sloane. *Of course.* He convulsively jammed down the detonator button. Morrigan cringed, but there was no result. She shifted her attention to the dwarf, but he was already running toward the casinos. "Appropriate." She shook her head and called, "See you next time, coward."

She knelt beside Sloane as he slumped to the ground, his breathing shallow and irregular. Her arrow hadn't come out the front, so she supported his shoulder with one hand to keep him from falling backward onto it. Ruby covered the six feet from the other fallen man to kneel on his other side and said, "How's it look?"

Morrigan replied, "He'll live, I think. As long as we get some ambulances in here, stat."

Demetrius asked, "Is it safe to do so?"

Ruby said, "Yeah, go ahead." She looked down at the man and sighed. "Quite the audacious plan, blowing up the casinos. You don't like to lose, do you?"

Something between a cough and a laugh came out of his mouth as he shook his head. "No, I do not. All you bastards had to do was let me build one casino here. Was that seriously too much to ask?"

Morrigan snorted. "They did their research on you, Mr. Sloane. Once you had a foothold, you would have made moves to take over the whole place. You're not historically kind to your business partners."

He nodded. "Maybe this time it wouldn't have been like that. I really wanted this. Wanted to go fully legit." He laugh-coughed again. "Well, as legit as a casino can be."

Ruby shook her head. "Well, you'll have a lot of time to imagine what it would have been like in prison, I guess."

Sloane's gaze shifted past her, and he shook his head, seeming sad but somehow still defiant. "No. I think I'd rather go out with a bang."

Morrigan caught the motion from the edge of her eye. She was reaching for an arrow in an instant, the most lethal of the bunch, the one she called the spinner. It was a tech arrow, designed so it traveled faster by spinning as it flew. She knew that to loose it meant death for the target in most cases, which was why she hadn't felt the need to use it before. She released it at the same moment Ruby dove at the man she'd downed, the man with one arm trapped in Idryll's mouth.

The other arm, though, the one with the artifact on it, was in motion toward them. The tentacles shot out of it, crossing the distance between them in no more than a second, and she screamed a futile warning to Ruby. It arrived too late, but it didn't matter. Goryo hadn't aimed the attack at her. His shadow magic assault speared through Sloane's throat, clearly severing all sorts of important things to judge by the way he immediately twitched and sputtered.

Her arrow took the man who had hurt Margrave in the face, ending him for good. She turned to Sloane, as did Ruby from her prone position near Goryo. He made one last convulsive jerk, then his eyes defocused. A series of loud sounds that could only be explosions came from the left side of the Strip, and Morrigan jerked her head toward the noise in time to see the Mist casino shudder, creak, and begin to collapse in upon itself.

She watched in horror as it cascaded down like a house of cards, damaging the Darkest Night casino next to it and shooting a column of dust up into the air. She had no words, couldn't put together any coherent thoughts in the aftermath of such wholesale destruction. In moments where emotion overcame her, she almost always did the same thing and turned to her sister for comfort.

Ruby couldn't offer it, though. Her body was locked like a plank, rigid and vibrating as if it would shake itself apart. Morrigan's mind babbled with terror at the sight of the octopus-shaped bracelet that was digging its way into the flesh of her sister's left forearm.

CHAPTER THIRTY

Ruby found herself in darkness with no idea how she'd arrived there. The space felt enormous and abandoned. *Am I dead? What happened?*

A low chuckle sounded from nearby, and she turned to see *Mirra* Kaeni stride forward, dressed as she'd seen her last, in shining chain armor with ebon plates over the top, both setting off the snowy white hair and pale skin to good effect. "No, you're not dead. You are simply inside your mind."

"You can read my mind here? Is that part of being the Mist Elves' ruler, or what?"

"No, that's a feature of your will. You are shouting out your thoughts. I cannot help but hear them. To the question of the ruler, the mystics are quite right. I accomplished a great deal during my time, but it was more often through coercion rather than agreement." She stepped closer, opening her arms wide. "Power, you see, is a baseline requirement. Once you have it, people are far more willing to agree to do what you request of them. Then, one can choose to be magnanimous in their dealings with others. It makes great, great works possible, the kind that benefits everyone and transforms societies."

Ruby sensed pressure on her senses. She'd experienced it before and had generated it once. "Nope, I think we'll stay in this setting, thanks. You know, what you describe sounds a lot like manipulation. Like how you're trying to manipulate me right now."

The other woman's tone changed, sounding far more unlike Ruby's memory of her as she spoke with a syrupy sweetness tinted with wheedling. "I had to test you. Make sure you were worthy, which you clearly are. You and I can be equal partners. Together, we will build our power in your world. Together, we will make amazing things happen, fantastic things that will benefit all the people."

Ruby shook her head. "I know you're not Kaeni. Get out of my head and show yourself."

A flash of light filled the space, doubtless a memory pulled from her battle with the mad Mist Elf, and an Atlantean stood before her. He was tall, dark, and haughty, with arrogance radiating from him. His black hair was bound in thick locks that fell over his shoulders and hung down nearly to his waist. He wore blue and green armor that appeared to be composed of individual scales, each perfect and shining, seeming to ripple as he breathed. He held a trident in his right hand, almost as tall as he was, and a weighted net in his left. "Very well."

Ruby rolled her eyes. "Wow. How stereotypical. Should I call you Aquaman and be done with it?"

He snarled, "We are the source of the stereotypes. When pitiful humans from long ago worshiped Poseidon and

Neptune, they were truly paying homage to us. As was, and is, right and proper."

Ruby crossed her arms and shook her head. "Yeah, whatever. Delusions of grandeur, I say."

He demanded, "*I* say you will follow my orders and submit yourself to me, or I will fill your world with pain."

She couldn't hold back a laugh. "Buddy, I *never* do what anyone says. That's kind of like my main thing."

"Perhaps a taste of that pain shall prove informative."

He pointed the trident at her and sent a blast of electricity cascading from it. She waved her hand, and it vanished, transforming into a shower of sparkles. "Please. If we're in my head, nothing's going to be decided by magic. Did you not learn even that little thing about me?"

He broke into an unexpected smile, and she realized he could be handsome if he weren't so malevolent. *Kind of like the devil in stories, I guess. My personal Asmodeus.* "Very well, then. Let's see what you're made of."

He rushed forward to battle her, and she dashed ahead to meet him. She expected him to throw the net, but he didn't, and her respect for his tactics shifted up a notch. *Better to wait until I'm not expecting it, obviously.* She kept her hands at the ready, and when he stabbed out the trident, it was a simple matter to dip slightly and bring her hand around in a circle to block the shaft, pushing the tips away from her.

She slammed a quick sidekick into his ribs, but he seemed unmoved by her martial display. He spun backward, leading with his elbow, and she dropped to the ground to strike at his knee. He twisted at the right instant, and her foot caught the back of the joint rather than the front or side. What might have cost a lesser opponent their balance only sent him into a cartwheeling disengagement. She rose, and he waited for her to find her feet. His tone suggested grudging respect. "You fight well. Perhaps we could be partners in truth. I'll admit my earlier offer was indeed manipulation. Now I see that you are worthy."

Energy flowed through her, and she realized the fighting hadn't drained her at all. In fact, she felt better than she had for some time. *This is pure. This is me, no one else. Man versus man. Well, okay, woman versus imaginary mythical prince of hell, but close enough.* She charged ahead without responding, and he tried the net. She cut to the side and rolled, almost avoiding it altogether. It snagged her foot, but she extricated herself before the weights could wrap all the way around and slow her.

He twirled the trident through a series of spins, its heaviness negligible in his hands, and surprised her by going for a smash with the finial on the end opposite the spikes. She leaned away to avoid it, and he lunged forward to compensate, extending it enough to catch her a painful blow on the cheek. Blood seeped into her mouth from her nose, and she laughed. She hadn't fought a battle so pure in forever, probably since the days of training with Keshalla before coming back to Magic City.

She scowled at the notion that returning to her hometown had soiled her somehow, then realized he was trying to play with her brain again. *For all the talk of a truce, which I would never accept anyway, if this bastard wins, I'll be his puppet. That won't be good for anyone, but most especially not good for those I love.*

She strode forward with purpose, intent on ending the

fight. He recognized the change in her attitude and shifted to a defensive posture, blocking her attempts to punch and kick him while snapping out his blows only when he could be sure of not overstepping. She feigned a wound, hoping he'd buy into it, but he smiled and continued. *Dammit, this could go on forever. I'm guessing I won't keep feeling strong for as long as he will since this is his domain, even if I have some influence on it.* She disengaged and tried to force the surrounding area into a different shape, recalling the mountaintop with its clean, cold purity, but failed to accomplish it.

Okay, I might be in trouble. As if the thought had summoned them, Shalia and Tyrsh appeared a short distance away. Her foe started at the sight of them and moved into position to defend against all three. Shalia stood with her arms crossed, shaking her head at the Atlantean. "Pathetic. Of all the potential venues you could try, this is your choice?" She gestured at the surrounding space. "No wonder your people lost their homeland."

Tyrsh added, "And seriously, a trident? I know it's historical and all, but it's so impractical. You know what's much better? A sword."

Her sword suddenly filled her grip, and she grinned. "Now, let's see what you're made of."

The Atlantean backpedaled as she rushed forward, stabbing with his trident in a series of thrusts to keep her at a distance. She sidestepped the first, spun away from the second, and smashed her blade against his weapon in a strength-on-strength block for the third. If the clash had been purely physical, she might have lost that particular contest, but in her mind, she flat out refused to. The clash opened him for a kick, and she stomped his knee, then whipped an elbow into his face as he fell.

She stood over him as he lay on the ground, writhing and bleeding. Then he stopped, looked up at her, and laughed. "Well done, Ruby Achera. We will do this again and again until you finally surrender and do as I say."

She shook her head. "Please review my earlier comments about how likely I am to do what *anyone* says, much less a scumbag like you. Also, anytime, anywhere, chucklehead."

She woke suddenly to find herself on the ground in the real world. The cool grip of her sword filled her hand, and Morrigan and Idryll stared down at her. She rasped, "Whoever gave me the sword, good call."

Idryll grinned widely. "My idea. Your sister would've never thought of it. Honestly, it's a wonder the two of you made it out of your childhood, given the lack of a single brain shared between you." Morrigan offered a rebuttal, including a couple of choice curses, and the verbal battle was on.

As the shapeshifter continued to add inventive insults to the list, Ruby smiled and closed her eyes, trusting her partners would keep her out of danger while she rested for a minute.

CHAPTER THIRTY-ONE

It took a full week before things were even marginally back to normal in Magic City. Ruby, Morrigan, Idryll, Demetrius, and Margrave celebrated Margrave's release from his sickbed by gathering at Gambler's Victory, one of the more expensive and not-subtly-named places in town. They were seated at a round table in the corner, and both Ruby and Morrigan maintained sound shields so no one could overhear them. They couldn't do much about lip readers but had no reason to think anyone would care to watch them at the moment, anyway.

Demetrius said, "Finally, she asks me out on a date but doesn't mention it's a group thing."

Morrigan teased, "Woo," filling it with insinuation. She waggled her eyebrows for emphasis.

He scowled at her. "Who's paying?"

Ruby replied, "Dralen, of course."

Margrave asked, "Is he aware of that fact?"

Morrigan shook her head. "Hell no." Everyone laughed together.

They made small talk during the appetizers, but by the time their entrées arrived, they had moved on to practical matters. Family-sized platters of pasta were passed around, along with the large stuffed pork chops the place was known for. *Carb city. Bring it on.* Ruby said, "Even with the major events and two of the bad guys shuffling off the mortal coil, nothing is over."

Margrave nodded. "Yeah. The PDA is already buckling down, and the security companies are sniping at each other as if there's going to be an all-out war for business."

Demetrius added, "Or an actual all-out war."

Morrigan observed, "You know, within twelve hours of the Mist collapsing, Sloane's widow filed paperwork to buy the site and build a casino."

Margrave asked, "Won't the Mist come back?"

Her sister shook her head. "The Sunshis feel that the next move against them will be straight-up murder to get the property, and they've decided they prefer to live. They're heading back to Oriceran, and the Council is buying the site from them and keeping it in trust until they decide what to do with it."

Margrave turned serious. "The family might be making the wisest choice. Maybe you three should consider doing the same."

A trio of head shakes answered him. Ruby said, "We're not going anywhere until Magic City is free of all these scumbags."

Idryll added, "Where she goes or doesn't go, I'll be at her side."

Morrigan grinned. "Not getting rid of me that easily, old man."

A smile replaced Margrave's momentary seriousness. "I guess it's time to start working on some new gadgets in earnest, then."

Ruby chewed and swallowed. "I have some ideas."

Her sister replied, "Stupid ones, as usual. I have much better ideas. Let's do mine first."

Idryll shook her head sadly. "See? Can we banish the children to the bunker for a week, please?"

* * *

Jared Trenton noted that where before there'd always been only one or two guards accompanying him and Grentham to the Reno penthouse, on this visit that number had increased to four. *I guess the wife is even more concerned with security than her husband was.* They were escorted into the living room, where Julianna Sloane sat on the couch awaiting them. He was used to seeing her in outfits that showed off her assets. Today, instead, she was dressed in a black business suit with a charcoal blouse and low heels beneath a skirt that reached almost to her knees. Her jewelry was elegant but understated, appropriate for a woman in mourning.

She gestured for them to sit and waited in silence while they complied. "You need to understand that my husband was obsessed with Magic City on a very personal level. It was something about being tormented by magicals when he was young. He was never willing to tell me the whole story, but it was a deep hurt that never healed. It colored everything he did there, despite my best efforts to provide perspective."

He nodded, and Grentham did the same, but he was unwilling to speak. Although she seemed sane and steady, he'd seen the wildness in her eyes and knew, if anything, she would be quicker to turn to violence than her husband had been.

Julianna thanked the tuxedoed servant that handed out three glasses filled with ice and vodka and sipped from hers. He followed suit because he had to, hoping she hadn't decided to poison them. She continued, "For me, it's not personal. It's business. The business of acquiring money, and influence, and ultimately, power. Make no mistake." She set the glass on the table and stared at them. "We will find a way into that city, and we will kill anyone we must to achieve that goal. My husband was obsessed, but his instincts were as sharp as ever. Ely offers opportunities that Vegas, Reno, or any other gaming center can't match. One of two things will happen: I will own the city, or I will reduce every bit of it to flaming wreckage."

She twisted her body slightly and locked her eyes on Grentham. "I've seen the footage of the event. You ran." The words came out like an accusation, and the dwarf flinched under her assault. "Still, nothing you could have done would have changed things at that point. So, while you have demonstrated a concerning streak of cowardice, you get to live and try to overcome it." Her chin raised a touch. "I believe we can all better ourselves."

Jared wondered where she'd come from, who she'd been before she met Sloane. *Something to investigate if I can figure out how to do so with complete and utter deniability.* Her gaze landed on him, and he forced himself to meet it. She said, "Your leash is a little longer than it was, but only slightly so. I'm bringing in help under my exclusive orders. You and your partner should concern yourself right now with gathering all the information available on the quickest and easiest way to turn the Council to our perspective. I presume it will involve killing several of them, which is acceptable. I need to know which ones if I'm to avoid the inconvenience and delay of doing away with them all."

She shook her head, appearing suddenly sad. "My husband was a sword. I am a scalpel. Both can get the job done." She stood, signaling that the meeting was at an end. "If they don't see it my way on the issue with the open plot that used to hold the Mist, we'll have to create a few more spaces ripe for new construction, won't we?"

The excitement increases as the story continues! Join Ruby and her friends in *THE HUNT IN MAGIC CITY*, coming May 3, 2021.

Stay up to date on new releases and fan pricing by signing up for my newsletter. CLICK HERE TO JOIN.

Or visit: www.trcameron.com/Oriceran to sign up.

If you enjoyed this book, please consider leaving a review. Thanks!

If you enjoyed this book, you may also enjoy the first series from T.R. Cameron, also set in the Oriceran Universe. The Federal Agents of Magic series begins with Magic Ops and it's available now at Amazon and through Kindle Unlimited.

FBI Agent Diana Sheen is an agent with a secret...

...She carries a badge and a troll, along with a little magic.

But her Most Wanted List is going to take a little extra effort.

She'll have to embrace her powers and up her game to take down new threats,

Not to mention deal with the troll that's adopted her.

All signs point to a serious threat lurking just beyond sight, pulling the strings to put the forces of good in harm's way.

Magic or mundane, you break the law, and Diana's gonna find you, tag you and bring you in. Watch out magical baddies, this agent can level the playing field.

It's all in a day's work for the newest Federal Agent of Magic.

Available now at Amazon and through Kindle Unlimited

Thank you for reading Book 4 in the Magic City Chronicles, and for continuing on to read these author notes! I can't believe how fast this series is flying by!

There's a discussion in writing circles about whether you're a "Plotter," or a "Pantser." One who plots (duh), vs. one who sets the scene and lets the characters lead wherever they will. It's kind of a false dichotomy, because to some degree we all do some of both, but it's true there's a general preference toward one or the other.

I'm a plotter. I set up overall points for a series, then outline each book in an excel spreadsheet with a sentence or two per chapter telling me what to do. Then, I expand those sentences right before I'm about to write, into a page or so of things to mention or do. Sometimes complete with dialogue, sometimes not.

But the thing about that is that the final version of that spreadsheet often winds up looking different from the one I started with, because the characters do take over sometimes. You get an idea, you write it down, and suddenly your plans have changed.

That happened more times in this book than in any I've ever written before. I knew I wanted the sword, the Rhazdon artifact, and the big finish. I didn't realize that the main villain wouldn't make it out of the book alive. I didn't plan to have Ruby infected with the Artifact. That stuff just tumbled out of me and was too good not to keep.

So, writing for me is a lot like reading. While I have an idea what's coming up next, it's always possible it will change. Which is beyond cool, right?

Anyway, I'm feeling the Federal Agents of Magic vibe again bigtime. My first thought on the next series is to go back to work with those characters, although Martha and Michael would have to buy in for that to happen. We'll see how that works out!

I made the mistake of buying *Civilization VI*. That game is too addictive for words. Stay away. Stay *far* away. After much effort I secured a PlayStation 5, not because I needed it but because something inside me was obsessed with the idea of *having* it. I'm not proud of that. But I have to say, *Spider-Man: Miles Morales* is gorgeous. I'm looking forward to seeing what *Avengers* and *Cyberpunk 2077* look like on it. Also, I bought *Gauntlet*, which I remember so fondly from my younger years, and am looking forward to making my kid play it. ("Blue Valkyrie needs food badly!")

Really enjoyed *Flack* on Amazon Prime Video, and finishing up the *Mandalorian* on Disney Plus. I'm still really confused about the pacing in that show. It's so great story-wise, but so incredibly slow. Still, nice to see Kara Thrace again! Next up: *WandaVision*, and then the next Marvel thing.

Hershey park in PA opens on April 2. The kid and I will be there if my writing is done on book 5 and the weather permits. I got my second vaccine shot, so I'm brave enough now to consider being out and about (fully masked, etc., I'm not a fundamentally healthy person).

Still rereading the entire "Foreigner" sequence by C.J. Cherryh to keep my brain under control. Eagerly anticipating *Ready Player Two* when I find time for it.

Before I go, if this is your first taste of my Urban Fantasy, look for "Magic Ops." I promise you'll enjoy it, and you'll get more of Diana, Rath, and company. You might also enjoy my science fiction work. All my writing is filled with action, snark, and villains who think they're heroes. Drop by www.trcameron.com and take a look!

Until next time, Joys upon joys to you and yours – so may it be.

PS: If you'd like to chat with me, here's the place. I check in daily or more: https://www.facebook.com/ AuthorTRCameron. Often I put up interesting and/or silly content there, as well. For more info on my books, and to join my reader's group, please visit www.trcameron.com.

Let's talk about vulnerability. Did everyone just cringe a little? Maybe just rolled your eyes? I get it and I feel the same. It seems to be my word for the year. I'd like to trade it and I'd like to master it, both at the same time.

Pretty standard for me. Kind of how I feel about parties a lot of the time. Want to be invited, don't always want to go. (But to my credit, go anyway, have a great time, wonder why I don't go more often – repeat.)

I'm sure lockdown has a lot to do with this life lesson that keeps coming up. (Lockdown, quarantine. Kind of the same thing.) I live alone with two dogs and there's only but so much TV I can watch. Eventually I had a lot of spare time on my hands and I got a good look at a lot of my life.

It's actually a really good life. Sorry, there's no real sad story here. It *used* to be more of a hot mess. (See past author notes for loss of everything I owned, lots of cancer, great comeback. You get the idea.) Lately, it's been pretty good except for maybe that whole 2020 in general thing.

Which brings me back to what I noticed and have even sought out others to work on – vulnerability.

The researcher and fellow Austinite, Brene Brown describes vulnerability as 'uncertainty, risk and emotional exposure'. All of those sound so risky, full of awkwardness and are absolutely necessary to have deep, meaningful relationships with friends, family or any kind of loved ones.

It's probably a good thing that vulnerability is required to make strong connections or else a lot of us wouldn't try it. Staying behind a few well-constructed walls of who we want to be seen as, minus the need to expose things I'm not sure about or worry aren't good enough sounds like a good idea.

Too bad it ends up holding people at arm's length and can lead to feeling lonely in a room full of familiar faces. The only way out is to risk being myself and trusting my tribe will find me.

They always do, you know.

As an added bonus, when I did finally risk it all and was myself, I got to know me a lot better too. These days when someone asks, what do you want to do, I actually have an answer.

But apparently there's a new layer to let go of that I've noticed over the past year. Some places where I have found ways to hold back, be quiet and resist talking about myself. Frankly, without quarantine, I think I may not have noticed. Then, to make sure I didn't talk myself out of looking at how to do more, I found some people who wanted to work on that same thing with me.

I only regret that occasionally.

So far, I have resisted progress on what looks like micro

steps with a lot of bluster and words. Good sign I'm on to something and just need enough courage to keep going to get results.

With quarantine easing and the world opening slowly back up again, I wonder what I will clear out and what new things I will find. More adventures to follow.

CONNECT WITH THE AUTHORS

TR Cameron Social

Website: www.trcameron.com

Facebook: https://www.
facebook.com/AuthorTRCameron

Martha Carr Social

Website: http://www.marthacarr.com

Facebook: https://www.facebook.com/
groups/MarthaCarrFans/

Michael Anderle Social

Website: http://lmbpn.com

Email List: http://lmbpn.com/email/

Social Media:

https://www.facebook.com/LMBPNPublishing

https://twitter.com/MichaelAnderle

https://www.instagram.com/lmbpn_publishing/

https://www.bookbub.com/authors/michael-anderle